Books by Jeremiah Healy

Blunt Darts
Right to Die
So Like Sleep
The Staked Goat
Yesterday's News

Published by POCKET BOOKS

SWAN DIVE

Jeremiah Healy

To Patricia,
With the hope
that you enjoy it,

Jeremiah Healy
October 4, 1997

POCKET BOOKS

New York   London   Toronto   Sydney   Tokyo   Singapore

This book is a work of fiction. Names, characters, places and
incidents are either the product of the author's imagination or are
used fictitiously. Any resemblance to actual events or locales or
persons, living or dead, is entirely coincidental.

POCKET BOOKS, a division of Simon & Schuster Inc.
1230 Avenue of the Americas, New York, NY 10020

Copyright © 1988 by Jeremiah Healy

Published by arrangement with Harper & Row Publishers, Inc.

ISBN: 0-671-74329-5

First Pocket Books printing June 1989

10 9 8 7 6 5 4 3 2

POCKET and colophon are registered trademarks of
Simon & Schuster Inc.

Printed in the U.S.A.

For Kate Mattes and Jed Mattes

ONE

◆

A breeze on a Thursday in June rustled the papers on my desk, but I was holding the only two pieces of afternoon mail that mattered. The first arrived in an envelope with the distinctive royal blue logo of the Boston Police, a reminder of my appointment at the department's pistol range the following Monday morning. In Massachusetts, you have to reapply every five years to retain a permit to carry a firearm, and in Boston that means requalifying on the targets. It's a good rule, and I called a friend of mine who's a police chief in the small suburban town of Bonham to see if he could meet me at his facility to practice. He and his wife were going away for the weekend, but he left word with the officer on duty to let me in on Saturday.

Next I read the annual form letter from the licensing section of the Department of Public Safety. It advised me that pursuant to General Laws, Chapter

147, Section 22, *et seq.*, my present ticket as a private detective expired in forty-five days. Between now and then, I had to submit the enclosed application for renewal and accompanying paperwork.

I glanced over the renewal, my head telling me it was easier to fill it out now, my heart saying I was a little tired of playing with forms today. The liquid crystal on the cheap digital clock showed only 3:10, and my head won out.

Next to "Legal Name in Full," I block-printed "John Francis Cuddy." Above "Date of Birth," I told the truth. For residence, the Back Bay condo I was renting; for business address, the Tremont Street office with two windows and a door in which I was writing. The form for your original license has spaces to list similar prior employment, for me just the military police and the claims department of Empire Insurance. Neither form has a line for marital status, which saved my having to specify "widower."

I dated and signed the renewal, attesting separately to the truth of the statements and my honor as a taxpayer. Drawing a check for the $500 annual fee (and remembering when it was only $400), I called my surety company, getting their promise to send me a continuation of my $5,000 posted bond in exchange for another hundred bucks of premium. Then I went to the wall and took down my current license from the "conspicuous place" where the law requires it to be displayed. After my previous apartment/office had been hit by arson, I'd had to apply for a replacement certificate. Next to "Reason for Needing Replacement," I'd written "Burned out." Then I'd decided that sounded psychologically questionable and substituted "Destroyed by fire."

I turned the metal frame from Woolworth's glass-side down on my desk and niggled free the stubborn cardboard backing. I slid the license out and carried it down the hall to the nice receptionist in the CPA firm. She reminds me of aunts who bake cookies, and she photocopied the license for me when none of the accountants was looking.

Returning to my own office, I gathered up the junk mail that had blown off the desk in the draft I'd caused opening and closing the door. I put the original of the license back in the frame and on the wall. Paper-clipping the renewal to the rest of the documents, I dropped the package on top of the box to await the bonding company's certificate.

This time, the clock said just 3:45. On a Thursday in June. A warm one at that. I thought about dialing Nancy Meagher at the district attorney's office, but I was already seeing her for dinner at her apartment in South Boston. We'd been back together, in my sense of the word, for only a few weeks, and I didn't want to push it. I also thought about driving to Southie a little early, but I'd visited the cemetery the day before, and Beth's hillside was just five blocks from Nancy's building.

I decided to lock up and go for a walk. Out into the sunshine across from the Park Street subway station at the corner of the Common. Past Old Granary Burial Ground, resting place of Samuel Adams and Paul Revere, where rubbings from the gravestones had to be prohibited because the copying also eradicates. Through Government Center, the utilitarian tower of the McCormack federal building in stark contrast to the massive, award-winning City Hall designed by I. M. Pei. And down into Quincy Market, Boston's refurbished waterfront, which has served as a model for a dozen such projects elsewhere.

The market area was vibrant as ever, the pillared and domed center building and cobblestoned walkways teeming with upscale urbanites drinking at the outdoor cafés and downscale tourists engaged in a perpetual feeding frenzy. You can hardly blame the tourists, given the variety of delights tactically placed around each corner they turn. Souvlaki stands, raw bars, fried dough counters. Mixed fruit on a stick, frozen yogurt atop a cone, shish kebab in a pita pouch. All elaborately festive and apparently successful, until you notice that a chocolate chip cookie costs as much as a loaf of bread in Omaha and that very few visitors wearing J. C. Penney shirts are toting bags from the tony designer shops crammed into ten-by-twenty stalls.

I appreciate what the market area has done for the city, but I can take it only in small, infrequent doses. At least the folks there that afternoon were laughing and alive, which was more than I could say for many of the people I'd been around lately.

"What's that?" I said, looking down at the kitchen floor.

Nancy Meagher closed the apartment door behind me. "A friend of mine wanted to adopt a dog, so I went up with her to an animal shelter in Salem. When I saw this little fella, I knew there was something missing in my life."

The tiny kitten, a gray tiger with too-big paws and ears, just stared up at me.

Nancy said, "Don't you want to know his name?"

"I could never see naming something that doesn't come when you call it."

"Oh, John. You're going to love him. Isn't that right, Renfield?"

"Renfield?"

"Yes. Ring a bell?"

"Not quite."

"In the Dracula movie with Bela Lugosi, Renfield is the Englishman who goes mad and begins eating small mammals for their blood."

I watched Renfield and wiggled my foot. He licked his chops and pounced, sinking his front claws and teeth into my sock, playing tug-of-war with the spandex.

"Why don't you two go into the living room. White wine okay?"

"Fine."

I dragged Renfield into Nancy's bay-windowed parlor and settled onto one of her throw pillows. Prying his grip off my foot, I hefted him in my palm. He was about the size and weight of a brandy snifter. He blinked at me once, then started gnawing on my thumb.

Nancy came in with our drinks. "Getting acquainted?"

"I think he senses you're running low on parakeets."

She set the glasses down and picked up a Ping-Pong ball. She tapped it with her fingernail, which got Renfield's immediate and undivided attention. Then she tossed it onto the hardwood floor at the edge of her rug. Renfield sprang from my hand and hit the ground with all legs pumping, catching up to the ball and whacking it till he and the ball skittered out of sight into the kitchen.

I reached for my drink and Nancy raised hers. We clinked as she said, "To a fresh start."

We cruised through the next half hour on simple, almost domestic small talk. I helped make a salad to go with the swordfish in the broiler, and we ate at her kitchen table. There was a persistent but erratic scratching at my pants cuff, like a determined novice lineman trying to climb his first telephone pole.

"Is it all right to feed him from the table?"

She smiled. "Softening already?"

I picked up a morsel of swordfish the size of my pinkie nail. "Just thinking of my wardrobe."

As soon as Renfield saw the treat, he sat up and begged. Well, as much as a cat will beg. I lightly dropped the food onto his nose, his pupils focusing crazily as he tentatively swatted and then gobbled it. I repeated the drill twice more.

"Why are you putting the food on his nose?"

"I like watching his eyes cross."

"Great," she said around a bite of tomato. "If the behaviorists are right, in two months I'll have a Siamese."

We finished dinner and moved into the parlor, dawdling over the rest of the wine as we watched the evening news. About halfway into the broadcast, the male anchor warned that the following scenes might not be suitable for young children. After a pause short enough to retain viewers but not long enough to shoo any kids out of the room, the female anchor introduced the videotape of a courthouse shoot-out involving me a few weeks before.

Nancy started to get up. "I'll change it."

"No."

She looked at me questioningly.

"No, Nance. I want to see it."

The video was disjointed, the camera operator near the witness stand obviously and understandably jumping and bumping the tripod as the gunfire erupted. The tape showed the situation from an angle I hadn't had in person.

Nancy said, "You're studying it, aren't you?"

I kept my eyes on the screen, the station rolling the footage in Sam Peckinpah slow motion. "Yes."

"Why?"

12

"To see if there was anything I could've done, anything I missed."

"So you're better next time?"

"In a manner of speaking." The program dissolved to a commercial. "Think it's crazy?"

"Yes. And no, I guess. I do the same thing after a trial, whether I get a conviction or not. I rerun the case in my head, to see if I can spot something I can use again. What I can't see is how you can do it when you were so emotionally involved."

"I can't explain it in words. It's more like I don't feel the emotion now, the incident separates from the lesson."

Nancy nodded, but I think less from being persuaded than from wanting to close the subject. To avoid her own similar memories of a wintery night in the graveyard around the corner. Instead she came over to me, resting her head on my shoulder.

I said, "You know, you're the best thing that's happened to me in years."

She moved her face very slowly, left to right, nuzzling me softly just above the collar. "I'd like to be more than that."

I tilted my head back just enough to see her. Bangs of short black hair and freckles sprinkled just right against a field of widely spaced blue eyes. "If our luck holds out, I think you're going to be."

"Would the smart money be on tonight?"

I sighed, and Nancy went back to my neck, where she pecked me once and said, "I didn't think so."

"Nance—"

"No." She pulled away, a little sheepish. "I'm sorry, I keep doing that. I meant that no, I understand. I was just looking for a status report, not trying to put on any pressure."

"I know. And I appreciate it."

She put both her hands on my shoulders and squeezed. "Boy, I just hope we're both worth waiting for."

We laughed. I said, "How about dinner tomorrow?"

A frown. "I can't. I promised a friend of mine from New York that I'd fly down on the shuttle tomorrow afternoon and stay the weekend with her."

"Monday then?"

"Sounds great."

"I'll pick you up at your office, and we can eat at Locke Ober's."

"Percy Plunger. Are we celebrating?"

"Anticipating."

She smiled. "Make it about six-fifteen. Whenever I break away early on a Friday, things pile up."

After the network news, I kissed Nancy goodnight and drove home to the eight-unit brownstone on Beacon Street. I parked my Fiat 124 in the assigned space behind the building, the lamp pole's light supposedly discouraging the car strippers that are a constant of downtown living. A couple of years ago, our state legislature passed a Home Defense bill, which basically gives a resident the right to shoot an intruder who the resident believes might cause serious injury or death. Now some of the gentry wanted a Blaupunkt Defense bill, which would allow the owner of a BMW to shoot any thirteen-year-old breaking into the car for the radio. I wouldn't bet against it.

Walking around to the front of my building, I got my mail from the entrance foyer and climbed the stairs to the condo. My landlord, a doctor on a two-year residency program in Chicago, had decorated the place with Scandinavian Design furniture. In daytime, the pieces were cheerily set off by the ultraviolet rays flooding through the seven living room windows. Now, however, I had to use the lights.

My home answering machine glowed one message in fluorescent green-on-black. I rewound the incoming cassette while I called my office answering service. The service said a friend of mine from college, a lawyer in Peabody, needed to speak with me. He was on the tape too as it replayed.

"John, Chris Christides. Jeez, I hate these things, you know, you never know how much . . . Anyway, they had you on the news, from the courtroom thing again. I'm in kind of a tight spot with one of my cases tomorrow, and I'd really appreciate your giving me a call tonight, anytime. Thanks."

I hadn't seen Chris in maybe four years. He was a third-string offensive guard on our Holy Cross team back when ability and heart meant a little more than size. He was only about five nine, but at two hundred he hit like a bowling ball with legs, blocking on sweep plays and specialty teams. Dialing his number, I thought also, and painfully, about his wife, Eleni.

"Hello?" said a familiar accented woman's voice.

"Eleni?"

"Yes? Who is this?"

Her words were more slurred than I remembered, but only a little more. A good sign, I hoped.

"Eleni, it's John Cuddy. Chris called me."

"Oh, John! It is good to hear the voice. How are you?"

"I'm well, thanks."

"John, I know Chris need to see you, but he is not here now. Can you come his office tomorrow, nine o'clock?"

"Do you have any idea what it's about?"

"No. I know Chris is very worried on this case, and if he talk to you, he could tell why."

I thought of asking her to have Chris call me back, but then I pictured her, the way she looked the last

15

time I'd seen her, and pushed away an image of what further progression of the multiple sclerosis had done to her by now. "I'll be there. He still in the building on Lowell Street near the courthouse?"

"No, no. He give that up, John. He have the office here in the house now. We fix up the garage."

I caught myself estimating mentally what Beth's last few months with the cancer would have done to our finances without Empire's hospital plan. I didn't want to think how Eleni's illness might have drained them. She gave me directions I half recognized, and we said good-bye.

Talking with her on the phone had quashed most of the good spirits left over from dinner with Nancy. I read more bad news in the *New York Times* for another hour or so, then went to bed early.

TWO
—◆—

I was up by 6:30, thumping over Storrow Drive on the Fairfield footbridge by 7:00. I headed downstream, favoring the waterside path over the roadside one.

People who say they can't stand running must never have jogged along the Charles River. I passed the giant layered bust of Arthur Fiedler, the late conductor of the Boston Pops. The mustached granite face eternally watches the Hatch Shell stage from across the field where thousands, over half a million at Fourth of July, would cheer for the orchestra and him. Near a scullers' boathouse, I almost collided with Robert Urich, practicing a firing stance with his .45 while filming a "Spenser for Hire" sequence on location. In the water, geese were landing, mallards were swimming, and cormorants were diving. What more can you ask from a sport?

I forded the river courtesy of the Museum of

Science and turned upstream on the Cambridge side, recrossing at the Massachusetts Avenue bridge. I went in the Bildner's food emporium near Commonwealth for muffins and orange juice. Back on the street, I saw a throng of well-dressed office workers waiting outside a shuttered video store. The air was chilly, and they were stamping around, flapping their arms and checking their watches like a line of addicts outside a methadone clinic.

At the condo, I showered, shaved, and debated what to wear. When I was an investigator at Empire, I talked with another classmate in Legal about throwing some simple cases Chris's way. Unfortunately, Chris was the kind of lawyer that dressed in nubby polyester sports jackets and ill-matched slacks. His files were coffee-stained and never contained the right documents in the proper order. In the words of the guy in Legal, it was one thing to wish Chris well but quite another to refer him an insured as a client.

I rummaged through the closet. While I didn't want to outshine Chris by wearing a suit, I also figured there was at least a chance I'd have to be in court with him that morning. I pulled out gray slacks, a blue blazer, and a conservative striped tie.

I drove to Route 1 and followed it north, mercifully opposite the choked, honking traffic crawling southbound into the city. Route 1 is a mixed bag of wholesome family restaurants, space-devouring businesses like fence companies and lumberyards, and pornographic adult entertainment centers. As I passed one, its marquee read: ALL NEW! "A HARD MAN IS GOOD TO FIND" AND "EVERYBODY COMES BETWEEN ME AND MY CALVINS."

I turned northeast at the Route 128 interchange, and then shortly thereafter took the exit for Route

114. After a mile and a half of suburban forks, I found the Christideses' house.

It was a small ranch on a quarter of an acre. I remembered when they bought it, to be their "starter" home. Back when her inability to conceive was thought to be a temporary aberration in an otherwise healthy woman. Then Eleni began to suspect that the infertility might be related to the occasional tremors she experienced in her legs. She nearly didn't mention them to her doctor, "they was such a small thing." After the tests and the retests came the confirmation. There was no relationship between the unsteadiness and the infertility, but the tremors were just the first signals of MS.

I left the Fiat curbside, even though the driveway had been widened to simulate a parking area for the converted garage. The new office appeared makeshift from the outside, not exactly the kind of facade that would inspire confidence in the professional working behind it. Chris's old sedan, a Pontiac that had two years on my coupe, slumped over the macadam abutting the space where the overhead door used to hang.

I knocked on a human-size entrance and heard Chris's voice say, "Yeah, come in."

The cramped reception area was paneled in bottom-of-the-line imitation pine that was already starting to yellow. I stepped around three molded plastic chairs of different colors and a low veneered coffee table with some ragged magazines. Chris stood at a desk that seemed secretarial but had no one behind it. He once told me that he was the first member of his family to go to college, much less law school. From what I remembered of his professional stature four years earlier, he was losing ground.

"John, John! Jeez, it's good to see you."

He hustled over to shake my hand, clutching and crushing a manila folder in his left fist. His curly black hair looked home-cut. Wearing a shirt whose collar points were a decade too long, he'd also put on thirty pounds that he didn't carry well.

"Chris, it's been a while. How's Eleni doing?"

His broad, mobile face drooped. "The best she can. With the MS, sometimes it's the muscles, other times the breathing or the voice. What can you do?"

He began to walk backward toward a half-opened door. "Come on into my office so we can sit. I got a temp that was supposed to be here twenny minutes ago, but you and I gotta talk quick if we're gonna be on time."

I figured he'd tell me for what.

"Chris, I don't do divorce cases."

"This isn't like a divorce case."

"Chris, you're representing this woman, right?"

"Hanna. Her name's Hanna Marsh."

"Hanna. And she's got a five-year-old daughter?"

"Right. Victoria. Vickie."

"And in an hour you're supposed to be in Marblehead at the office of the attorney for Hanna's husband to discuss things like custody, support, and division of property?"

"Well, yeah, of course things like that, but—"

"Chris, that sounds a hell of a lot like a divorce case to me."

Chris whoofed out a breath and held up both his hands. "Jeez, John, will you just let me tell it all the way out first?"

"All right."

"Then you can make up your mind."

"I said all right. Go ahead."

"All right." Chris collected himself, opened the file, then closed it again. "Aw, I don't need the details to tell you the way it is. This Hanna, she and her husband live—lived, the husband's still there—in Swampscott. She moved out on him and took the kid with her. Somehow she ends up at the doorstep of this woman that I represented some years back in *her* divorce but never charged."

"Never charged?"

"Billed, billed. Never billed. I used to do a lot of kinda courtesy stuff for family and friends in the Greek community here and there, you know? You're in solo practice, you gotta do those kinds of cases to get the better ones, the bigger ones later."

"Go on."

"Anyway, this former client's got an apartment to rent, and I guess Hanna musta seen it in the paper. Hanna's from Germany, met her husband when he was in the army over there, and she hasn't got any relatives over here. Truth is, she ain't got a pot to piss in, but Nerida—that's my former client—she sees Hanna and the little kid and, well, she takes 'em in, cat and all."

"Cat?"

"Yeah. The little kid, Vickie, she's got a cat, kitten, whatever."

"I don't see—"

"So, Hanna and Vickie are in the crummy first floor of the three-family here while the husband, his name's Roy, Roy Marsh, lives in a waterfront contemporary he had built over there in Swampscott."

"And you're representing Hanna against him."

"We already established that."

"Chris, it still sounds like a divorce to me."

"Just wait, just wait a minute, okay?"

I looked at him but didn't talk.

"You see, I don't need you to do any investigating here. I mean, like assets or peephole stuff or like that. This guy Marsh is loaded, and I've got him dead to rights on at least one solid affair with a nurse who works Samaritan Hospital. This nurse, you wouldn't believe it, is off Mondays and Tuesdays yet, perfect for screwing around, huh? Plus Hanna says he's done God knows how many pickups, hookers even."

"You've got him financially and morally, where do I fit in?"

Chris shifted his eyes down and away from me, fiddling with a ballpoint that had printing on its side, a giveaway advertisement from some bank. "He scares me, John."

I watched Chris until I realized I was making him uncomfortable. "What do you mean?"

"Just that. You think it's easy for me to say?" Chris squirmed in his chair, rubbing his left knee. His "civilian-preservation" knee, he called it senior year of college, the injury that kept him out of the draft's chilly grasp. "The guy scares me."

"Has he done something?"

"Not exactly."

"Well, threatened you, what?"

Chris glanced up at me, not liking this at all. "Nerida, this former client, she calls me and pours out Hanna's sob story. Then Nerida calls Eleni, and tells her, and so Eleni nags at me till . . ." Chris gestured at the folder. "Look, I'm not complaining. This is a good case. Jeez, maybe a dream case, the guy's earning power. But this Marsh, as soon as he hears I'm gonna represent his wife, he comes in here, to my office. Nobody out in reception that day, he comes in, stands in that doorway there, and just looks at me."

"Looks at you?"

"Yeah, just looks at me. I know he was doing it

before I looked up from what I was working on, because I could feel the guy staring down at me. Anyway, he looks at me, and when I ask him what he wants, he says, 'I just wanted a look at you. I just wanted a look at the man who thinks he's gonna take away everything I've worked for.' He wasn't yelling. Jeez, he didn't even say it angry or nothing. Just low and even, like he was some gunslinger in a western. He stared and said that, and left. He didn't even tell me his name, like automatically I'd know who he was."

"Did you?"

"Did I?"

"Did you know it was Roy Marsh?"

"Oh, yeah, Hanna described him to me. She's afraid of him, too. Along with everything else, it seems he was a little free with his hands."

"Can't you get the court to order him not to bother you? Or Hanna?"

"In a general sort of way, yeah. But we're not at that stage yet."

"I don't follow you."

"Well, we haven't filed for divorce yet, so there's nothing for the court to order him on."

"Why don't you file?"

"There's a thirty-day separation requirement, and Hanna only moved out a coupla weeks ago. I could go to court and get that waived, but in these things it's usually better over the long haul to avoid ruffling feathers."

"Meaning, don't make the other side mad in the short run by having court orders against him?"

"Right."

"And try to settle out of court first."

"Yeah. Well, kinda. See, if we can negotiate a fair settlement out of court, then we can put all the kinds of things I'd want the judge to order in our written agreement, and then we just pass it by the court at the final hearing."

"So everything looks like a consensus, not a command?"

Chris beamed. "Couldn't have put it better myself."

"Okay, let me get this straight. You're afraid of Marsh, but you don't want to tick him off by going to court first. So you want me to do exactly what?"

"Come with me, with Hanna and me, to the settlement conference over to Roy's lawyer."

"And do what?"

"Nothing. Just sit there."

"Chris, you want a bodyguard."

He winced. "I wouldn't call it that."

"I would. Why don't you hire an off-duty cop?"

"Because the coupla guys I know on the Peabody force would be out of their jurisdiction in Marblehead. And I don't know anybody on their force."

"Then why not have the settlement conference here?"

Chris slouched back in his chair, placing his palms behind his head and grinning. "Because, as a negotiating tactic, I let her persuade me to have it in Marblehead."

"Hanna?"

"No, no. Felicia Arnold. She's Roy's attorney. Heard of her?"

"No."

Chris closed his eyes and spoke blissfully. "She's big-time, John. Used to do a lot of criminal defense work, then got religion and does world-class divorce stuff. It proves that this guy Marsh is the real thing, financially speaking."

I thought about Chris and how much this case probably meant to him and Eleni, "financially speaking." I thought about how I had lost Beth, a day at a time over months, while Chris was losing Eleni, a day at a time over years. I had agreed to do dumber things for worse reasons.

"Okay, I'm in."

Chris came forward, wringing his hands like a big winner about to rake in a poker pot. "Great, great."

"Are we meeting Hanna there?"

"Naw, her car's on the fritz, so I picked her up this morning. She and the kid are with Eleni. In the kitchen. C'mon."

As Chris grabbed his coat off the hook behind the door, I said, "By the way, what does this marauder do for a living?"

Chris balked. "Marsh?"

"Yeah, Marsh."

Chris turned away and began walking. "He sells insurance."

She looked worse than I could have imagined.

Hanna Marsh stood up when Chris and I entered the kitchen. She rose a good inch taller than Chris, even in flat shoes. A sturdy figure that childbearing had made a little fleshy. She wore her platinum hair short enough to show dark roots if there had been any. A blond girl clutched the woman's right leg at the knee with both arms, causing Hanna's simple blue wool dress to bunch up. The child first buried her face in Hanna's thigh, then looked up at me bright-eyed and said, "My name's Vickie, and this is my mother."

I tried to manage a convincing smile at both of them, but Eleni's appearance had shocked me. A doctor friend once told me that multiple sclerosis waxes and wanes. For Eleni, it looked like straight-line deterioration.

I recalled her first with a cane, then metallic polio braces. Now the MS had shoved her into a wheelchair.

The hands and arms looked normal, but whatever was left of her legs was hidden in folds of a long black skirt, and there was an intermittent twitch in one of the muscles in her left cheek, creating the bizarre impression of a woman caricaturing a flirtatious come-on. The hair had grayed unevenly and seemed dried and pulled. Had you seen her from the neck up, and without the twitch, you might have called her a striking woman of sixty. If I had my dates right, she'd just turned thirty.

I looked for traces of the laughing, dancing woman of eighteen that Chris had introduced as his "arranged" fiancée. A black-haired, green-eyed immigrant whose independence wasn't much tempered by an almost complete inability to speak English. She'd come to America to avoid the restrictions of the old ways on what women could do and what men could do to them, but the disease had bowed her in a way that millennia of tradition hadn't.

"John," said Eleni.

I leaned over and took her hand, kissing her lightly on the cheek. "Thank you," she whispered into my ear.

Chris said, "Although it's pretty obvious, I guess, John Cuddy, Hanna Marsh."

"And me," said Vickie.

"And you," I said, looking down at Vickie as I shook Hanna's hand. It was dry, but trembling.

"Mr. Cuddy," said Hanna, her voice husky and catching, "I am sorry, but I want to thank you for coming with us today."

"Mrs. Marsh . . ."

"Hey," said Chris, "what's with this Mr. and Mrs., huh? It's John and Hanna, right?"

"And Vickie," I said, beating the child to it by just a bit, which seemed to please her.

26

"Where are we going, anyway?" said Vickie.

"Not you," said Eleni, gracefully, "You and me stay here and make the files. Remember?"

"Oh, right," said Vickie. She looked up and beckoned me to squat down to her level. "John, when you and Mommie get back, I want you to meet Cottontail."

"Cottontail?"

"Yes, she's my little kitty and she'd like to play with you."

"She would, huh?"

"Uh-huh."

"Well, we'll see if we have time afterwards. Okay?"

Vickie was crestfallen. "That's what my daddy always says. 'We'll see.'"

Chris said, "Hey, let's get rolling here." He moved to Eleni and bent down as if to kiss her, but I don't think they made actual physical contact. "We'll probably be there awhile, so be sure to give her lunch, huh?"

"Don't worry about us. Me and Vickie gonna be office people together. Right, Vickie?"

"Right."

Making the files and office people together. As Chris, Hanna, and I walked out to his car, I wondered whether the temp-being-late line was the only white lie he'd fed me.

THREE

♦

We drove east on Route 114, through the city of Salem, where witches were tried and burned, and past the state college. I rode in the backseat, listening to Chris and Hanna in the front. He was shooting disconnected questions rapidly; she was answering them as best she could. Based on what I knew about lawyer-client relations, most of the financial, custody, and even more personal topics Chris asked about should have been covered much earlier and without a third party like me present.

Chris had scrawled some directions to Felicia Arnold's office on a yellow legal pad, but once in downtown Marblehead itself, we got lost anyway. As Chris inched through the traffic patterns, the scenes out the windows supported my memories of Marblehead. One-way streets and narrow alleys, flanked by huge clapboard houses on postage-stamp lots.

Once the home port of ship captains, the town was

now headquarters for at least three distinct populations. One was the old-towners, enjoying substantial ancestral money and spectacular homes across the sheltered harbor on a spit of land called Marblehead Neck. The second group consisted of established, blue-collar families involved in commercial fishing or boat servicing. New-towners comprised the third population, mostly professionals who worked in Boston but had tired of city life and come to Marblehead to enjoy the sights and smells of a suburb on the sea. Word had it that some folks had done very well in the import business, specializing in a certain brown-green, vegetablelike substitute for tobacco.

Chris finally found Arnold's address, a beautifully restored two-story mansion on a high hill overlooking the harbor. Outside the car, the sea breeze lifted the high, metallic singsong of the masts and stays of thousands of pleasure sailers moored below us. At an average length of twenty-four feet and an average cost of $15,000, there was probably more seaworthiness there than we lost at Pearl Harbor.

A receptionist greeted us inside the heavy brass-knockered front door and led us upstairs. I was last in line, and as I reached the top of the steps, I saw off in a desk area to my right a svelte woman, fortyish with auburn hair clipped in a not-quite-punk style. She arched an eyebrow and smiled at me. A younger, lawyerlike man with tinted eyeglasses and a beard appeared beside her. She said something to him out of the side of her mouth while she watched me. I had the distinct feeling of being inspected and assessed as her smile became a smirk. The young man glared at me and turned away from her.

"Sir?" said the receptionist at my left.

"Yes?"

"The conference room is this way."

"Yes, thank you."

She showed me into a lushly carpeted arena with a glass-walled vista of sails so bright I had to squint. Chris and Hanna were already seated. Chris had both hands in his battered briefcase, coaxing a slim file past a bulging one. Hanna fidgeted next to him.

The receptionist said, "Ms. Arnold will be with you shortly" and closed the door.

Chris slapped a form in front of Hanna that had a slew of dollar figures in pencil, some of them with question marks and others crossed out and rewritten. "This is your financial statement."

Hanna's mind took a moment to click in. "I'm sorry, what?"

"Your financial statement. Weekly expenses and stuff you need like we talked about on the phone. It's just a draft, but we'll be using it today and you gotta make sure it's accurate."

Chris turned back to his file, madly flipping through it for something. Any fool could see that Hanna, who spent all of five seconds on the financial statement, was in no shape to verify anything, especially without her checkbook and bills for comparison. I also couldn't believe that Chris intended to show an opponent the uncertainties the hand-scratched form suggested about Hanna's, and Vickie's, needs.

There was a polite tap at the door, and my inspector/assessor came in. Up close, she seemed nearer to fifty and as carefully restored as her offices, with taut facial features, a glowing tan, and flattering highlights in the auburn hair that I somehow didn't think came from the sun. She smiled at all of us, lingering on me before saying, "Hello, Chris. And you must be Hanna. I'm Felicia Arnold."

Arnold extended her hand, with long, lacquered

nails, to Hanna, who shook, both figuratively and literally. Arnold turned to me and said, "I don't believe I've had the pleasure?"

I stood and said, "John Cuddy. I'm—"

"He's my new associate," Chris blurted.

I tried to keep the anger off my face as Arnold took my hand, then drew a nail along my palm as she released it, saying, "I'll have to follow your recruitment technique more closely, Chris. I hadn't realized you were expanding."

He said, "It was kinda sudden."

Before I could think of an acceptable way to tell the truth, Arnold swung her head around to bring everyone into the conversation. "I'm afraid I've just had a call from Mr. Marsh. He's been delayed and won't be here for approximately forty-five minutes."

Chris said, "Jeez, Felicia, I told you when we set this up that I'd be pressed if we ran late. I got this closing up in Lowell . . ."

Arnold acted heartbroken. "Yes, Chris, I know. And I reminded Mr. Marsh of that and he promised to be just as quick as he could be. But I really am reluctant to start anything substantive without his being present. So . . ." She opened the door and backed through it. ". . . I'm going to try to get some other work done. Please feel free to use the library. Just buzz five on the intraoffice phone if you'd like coffee."

After the door closed, Hanna said, very quietly, "I told you this would happen."

"Now, Hanna, I'm sure . . ."

I said, "What do you mean?"

Hanna looked up at me, her gray eyes hard and sad at the same time. "This is Roy's way. To hold everybody up so he can be the center, the control of everything."

"Well, at least this way you and Chris have more time to prepare. I'll be in the library so you two can talk confidentially."

I was scanning the library shelves for anything remotely interesting to read when I heard Arnold's voice behind me. "John, could I have a word with you? In my office?"

By the time I had turned around, she was already walking away from me with that long, vibrating strut of a leggy woman in high heels. I felt like a fourth-grader being summoned by the principal.

Arnold's office was a little larger than the conference room and even more tastefully appointed in Orientals and leathers. On the corner of the building, one large window captured the harbor while the other offered a more specific view of a couple of magnificent homes across the water on Marblehead Neck.

"Please, sit down."

I sat and watched her ease into the large swivel desk chair. She had a dancer's body and a ballerina's absolute control of it. I decided to wait her out.

"Well?" she finally said.

I just watched her.

She dissolved to disgust. Picking up the telephone, she pushed one button and said, "Paul? Now, please."

She hung up and seconds later a door on a side wall opened. The bearded man I'd seen earlier came through it, pad in hand.

Arnold said, "Mr. Cuddy, this is my associate, Paul Troller. Paul?"

Troller spoke without reading from his pad. "The Board of Bar Overseers lists no 'John Cuddy' or variation thereof licensed to practice in the Commonwealth. The Board of Bar Examiners shows no such name or variation sitting for any of the last three bar exams." He regarded me in a superior way. "I haven't had time to research the penalty for impersonating an attorney."

I said to Arnold, "His batteries expensive?"

She toyed with a grin as he clenched his free fist and bent the pad lengthwise in the other. "I wouldn't upset Paul if I were you. He was a finalist in the Golden Gloves before enrolling in law school."

I reached for my identification as Paul took a step toward me. "I'm a private investigator. There was some concern about Mr. Marsh's good behavior here today. If Chris had seen a copy of Paulie's résumé, I'm sure I wouldn't have been necessary."

Troller's next step was cut short by her saying "Paul," stretching out the syllable with an authoritative lilt at the end. She leaned forward and took my identification, seeming somehow relieved as she read it.

"You were the one involved in the shooting at Middlesex last month."

"Correct."

She glanced down at the ID again as she returned it to me. "That still your address?" She was leering at me and peripherally checking for Paul's reaction. Lovely woman.

I stood up. "Just call us when Marsh arrives."

He didn't look like an insurance salesman. What he looked like was a snake.

Marsh came into the conference room dressed in old corduroy pants and a windbreaker with a chamois workshirt underneath. He had black hair, short but shaggy, with the kind of wispy mustache that insecure nineteen-year-olds affect just after basic training. In his thick-soled "tanker" boots, he was three inches over my six two plus, but he was too lean and bony, as if someone had siphoned the flesh off him.

Arnold said, "Roy, I believe the only person you don't know is Mr. Cuddy. John Cuddy, Roy Marsh."

Marsh sniffed and said, "Who's he?"

I'd already prepared Chris for Arnold's reply. "Mr. Cuddy is a private investigator looking after Hanna's interests."

Marsh looked at me and sniffed again. "You got any ID?"

I showed him. His mannerisms were herky-jerky. I couldn't read his eyes because of the opaque lenses on the aviator sunglasses he wore, but I had a pretty good idea what I'd see in them, especially if I could check for cartilage holes up his nostrils as well.

Cocaine. And lots of it.

Handing back my identification, he grinned at Hanna, who looked down. "How you plan on paying for him?"

Chris reddened but didn't say anything. Marsh said, "He sees those stretch marks, he won't be too much interested in your interests anymore."

Chris coughed and said, "Felicia, I really gotta make that closing. Can we—"

"Just hold on, boy! This is my financial future we're going to be talking about, and I want things done nice and slow and right. So we all know where we stand. Got it?"

It was pretty obvious where Hanna stood. But Chris was the lawyer, not me.

Arnold said sweetly, "Roy, why don't you pull up a chair and we can get started."

Marsh having seized the iniative, Arnold exploited it. In detail, she went over Roy's financial statement, all typed out with elaborate exhibits. She even managed not to laugh when Chris produced his version of Hanna's financials. As the talk centered on Marsh's income, Roy looked bored. I don't think I would have been bored.

According to Arnold, Marsh made over $200,000 in each of the last three years working for the Stansfield Insurance Agency. That built the waterfront house at 13 The Seaway in Swampscott, for which Arnold had a written, certified appraisal of $150,000 against an outstanding mortgage of $40,000. The appraisal seemed low to me, but there was more to come: the BMW 633i that Marsh leased; the Escort station wagon, purchased for cash, that Hanna had taken; a twenty-six-foot inboard motor racer bought entirely on time; a snowmobile and trailer; and thousands of dollars of video and stereo equipment, hunting rifles, and club memberships. Rampant consumerism, but no real investments. Life in the fast lane.

Chris looked at his watch and wanted to start talking about more immediate things, such as temporary support, but he had let Arnold set the conference agenda and now she insisted, gently but firmly, on sticking to it. I suspected Marsh's late arrival had more to do with negotiating tactics than any business commitment he had, and Arnold's approach confirmed it. She was forcing Chris, because of his other appointment, to plod through the property stuff first, getting those long-term important matters resolved to Marsh's advantage before even considering the short-term issues.

Arnold represented that Marsh was maintaining $250,000 in life insurance payable to Hanna for the benefit of Vickie. Chris didn't scrutinize the certificate Arnold waved at him. Stupid. A guy in the business like Marsh could easily hoke one up. Chris should have realized that and insisted on a letter directly from the insuring company itself, postmarked at home office.

Then Arnold committed Marsh to paying Chris's legal expenses ("Would ten thousand be satisfactory, Chris?" "Ten . . . oh, yeah, sure, so long as we don't gotta go to trial over anything." "Oh, I'm sure we won't. We're all reasonable people here"). Roy was getting more bored, and impatient too, I expect because he had other things elsewhere that he wanted to deal with now that he didn't need to worry about Chris's efforts on his wife's behalf.

Marsh, however, had underestimated Hanna.

Just as Chris was about to agree that Hanna would trade her half of the house for a cash buy-out of $55,000, Hanna spoke for the first time. "No."

Chris and Arnold stopped talking. Marsh's head snapped to attention.

Arnold said, "But Hanna, the fifty-five thousand represents a fair share. It's half of the hundred-fifty fair market value minus the mortgage of forty."

"Yeah," said Chris, "see, it's half the equity in the house."

Hanna stared down at her hands, clamped together and whitening on the table top. "No. The house is worth more, much more than that."

Arnold said, "But Hanna, we have an appraisal."

Hanna said to Chris, "Do we have an appraisal?"

"Well, no, we don't. But jeez, Hanna, this here is from a reputable real estate firm."

Hanna said, "You ever have business with them before?"

"Well, no . . . but—"

"Then I want an appraisal, too."

Marsh started to say something but Arnold said,

"Certainly, Hanna. If that's what you want, I can easily commission another firm to do one. I must say though—"

"No."

"No?"

Hanna motioned at me. "No, I want the other appraisal from somebody Mr. Cuddy picks."

Each person turned to look at me, and I thought, "That's just swell."

Marsh said to me, "Just who the hell do you think you are?"

Arnold said, "Hanna, I'm sure Mr. Cuddy wouldn't be familiar with—"

"I trust him." No missing the implication there.

Marsh glared at her and started to say, "If you think . . ."

I said, "What harm could it do?"

Marsh whirled over to me and ripped off the aviator glasses. His pupils contracted from tea saucers to pinpoints. "The fuck asked you?"

I said, "Marsh, which hand do you write with?"

"What?"

"Which hand do you use when you write?"

Nobody else said anything. Marsh put his glasses back on with his left hand.

I said, "My guess is you're a lefty. That right, Hanna?"

"Yes."

"The fuck you want to know that for?"

"Because my dad always told me never to break the hand a man writes with. Especially here, since that'd restrict your making money and signing support checks and all."

Marsh started flexing his fingers, then caught himself.

Arnold said wearily, "Could we all drop this macho posturing for a while and return to business?"

Marsh let her save face for him, sagging back into his chair and folding his arms. He looked up at the ceiling as he said in a low voice to Hanna, "You really ought to take the fifty-five, honey."

Hanna said, "I want the house. The house itself."

Marsh bolted forward and I got ready. He yelled, "You what?"

Hanna's voice quavered but she pressed on. "That is the home that Vickie knows. Where she has grown and has her friends. This divorce thing is already hard for her. She should get to stay there with her mother."

Marsh slammed both his palms on the table and rose halfway out of his chair. "You fucking greedy bitch!"

Arnold said, "Roy, please—"

"The fuck you letting her get away with here? That house is mine! Goddamn it, I built that house. Every fucking board and nail came from money I earned, busted my ass for while she sat around trying to learn English off the soap operas and embarrassing me in front of my friends and contacts." He sank back down and refolded his arms. "No fucking house, and no fucking appraisal by Mr. Shitface here."

Arnold said, "Why don't we move on to—"

"Move fucking on all you want. The house stays with me, and the offer just dropped to fifty, and it's not looking too steady there, either."

Chris said, tentatively, gaugingly, "Hey, hey, we can come back to the house, all right? Felicia, how about the temporary support now?"

Hanna was crying. Not making any more noise than labored breathing requires, but both eyes were pinched closed and tears were sliding down her cheeks and onto the table. Arnold pulled open a drawer in the console behind her and lifted out a box of Kleenex. Daintily setting the box next to Hanna, Arnold touched her arm to suggest taking some.

Hanna stabbed at the box. Felicia, pretending to read Chris's handwritten financial statement, said, "I'm afraid the support's going to be a tough one, Chris."

"I'm really sorry about this, Hanna, but I already postponed this closing thing twice, and the bank attorney'll kill me if I'm not at the Registry by two-thirty."

Chris rolled up the window and pulled away, leaving Hanna and me standing on a street corner in Salem. We were only a short hop by cab from Chris's house in Peabody, and I wanted Hanna to get a chance to compose herself and have something to eat before she saw her daughter. On the ride from Marblehead, it had been decided that I'd give Hanna and Vickie a lift home. Chris had spent most of the ride gloating over what a great deal he'd worked out on everything but the house, which he thought Hanna should "rethink." I was a less than objective observer at the conference, but in my opinion Arnold had stolen Chris's pants without undoing his belt. The problem was it was Hanna's, and Vickie's, future that was on the line.

We found a small French restaurant called the Lyceum. With exposed-brick walls and high windows and ceilings, it was a pleasant and airy place to hold a postmortem. It being the end of the lunch hour, a few words whispered by me to the hostess got us a nice table away from the boisterous Friday hangers-on ordering one more carafe of the house white. I was pretty sure that if things couldn't be settled, Hanna and Roy would be litigating their differences in the Essex County Family and Probate Court a few blocks away.

I tried to make small talk for a while, but received only nods and one-word replies. Finally Hanna said, "Thank you for trying to help."

"You handled a difficult time well."

She nudged the remains of a large spinach salad around with a fork. "What do you think I should do?"

"Change lawyers by sundown" was what I thought, but it wasn't my place to say it. "It seems to me that the house, even without seeing it, is probably worth more than the appraisal said. I also think you're right to want to have it all, especially for Vickie's sake."

"My husband . . ." She almost smiled. "I must stop calling him so. Roy is a bad man to push like that."

"Just what kind of man is he, really?"

She hooded her eyes. "The kind you don't tell to do things unless you can beat him."

I considered asking her a lot about old Roy, but I had hired on as bodyguard, not psychotherapist. We closed out lunch by my promising to press Chris to get a second appraisal of the marital home.

We got a taxi on the corner and rode to Chris's house. The cab had no sooner pulled away than Vickie came bounding out the front door, laughing and calling, "Mommie! Mommie! Wait till you see what Eleni and I made!"

Inside the kitchen, Vickie proudly displayed the file folders they had assembled and the tray of baklava they had made. We each had a slice of the sweet pastry while Hanna kept her daughter focused on the morning with Eleni and away from the conference in Marblehead.

As Hanna went with Vickie to gather her things for the ride home, Eleni tugged on my sleeve.

"Things, they go well?" she said, without much confidence.

"No violence. A tough negotiation, but I'm no expert at judging lawyer talk."

Eleni rested her forehead in the palm of a hand. "When the husband come here, I see him. He smile at me when he leave. Not a nice smile, John."

"I've seen it."

"And not a nice man, John. Not just bad. He have the look."

"The look?"

"The look of the men I leave Greece to get away from. A man who does the gambling, visits the whores, beats the wife. The look of a man who like to hurt."

I could hear Hanna and Vickie coming back into the room behind me. Eleni said, quietly but insistently, "Watch good for them, John. Chris, he . . . cannot."

We got in my car, Vickie pleased with the ancient bucket seats fore and aft. She babbled on the way kids do, about her friends in Swampscott ("There's Ginny, and Karen, and Fred, but nobody *ever* wants to play with him"), her cat ("I know Cottontail's kind of a funny name for a kitty, but she's all white all over, and . . ."), her starting kindergarten in the fall ("I hope Fred's not in my class, but I don't know how they do things like that"). Ordinarily, I can't abide kidnoise, but it was nice to have something filling the air.

We arrived at the dilapidated three-decker and Vickie said, "Oooooh, wait till you see Cottontail! You'll love her, too."

Before I had turned off the motor, Vickie was out of the car, urging her mother to hurry. Once in the building foyer, Vickie ran to their apartment door.

"Cottontail? Cotton? We're home!" She put her ear up to the discolored wood and concentrated. "I can hear her crying. She must have missed us. It's okay, Cottontail, we're coming."

Hanna put the key in the lock, and Vickie burst in, calling the cat's name and getting a mewling sound from the back. "Oh, she must have got all tangled up again." She darted down the hall.

Hanna said, "You like something to drink, maybe?"

"No, I—"

The screaming cut me off. Hanna veered and raced the way her daughter had. "Vickie! Vickie!"

I caught up with them at the entrance to a rear bedroom. Vickie's face was burrowing into her mother's stomach, her screams muffled by Hanna's dress. Hanna's eyes were closed, and she was saying, "Don't look, don't look."

I pressed by them into the room. Although the wallpaper was dingy and scaly, there were some bright yellow curtains around the window and a yellow blanket covering the twin-size iron frame bed. The window itself had a pane of glass missing, and the broken shards were scattered on the sill, bed, and floor. But that wasn't the major damage.

Centered on the bed was a stained white kitten. The stain was red, from the blood that was still seeping into the blanket. Someone had taken a knife to the creature, peeling back its fur to expose musculature, bone, and an organ or two where the blade had slipped.

Cottontail looked up at me, squeezed its eyes shut, and let out a heartrending yowl.

FOUR

I called the Peabody police emergency number. The sergeant on duty said he thought the closest animal hospital was in Saugus. I dialed the hospital and was told to bring the kitten in immediately. Hanna wrapped Cottontail in the blanket, and I drove with flashers and horn while the cat cried on Hanna's lap in the front seat and Vickie cried in the back.

A veterinarian with long brown hair and warm brown eyes met us at the door. She pointed toward an admissions desk and rushed the cat into a back room. Hanna tried to comfort Vickie in the reception area while I filled out the paperwork. The woman behind the counter graciously allowed me to use her phone. I called the Peabody police back and provided some details on the break-in. They said they'd send someone that evening. Then I got the number for the Middlesex North Registry of Deeds in Lowell and punched it in. I told the paging operator there that it was an emergency.

About a minute later, Chris said, "This is Christides. Who is this?"

"John Cuddy, Chris."

"What the hell's the emergency?"

I told him.

"Jeez, John, I don't know what I can do about that."

I must have looked at the telephone receiver as if it were an alien artifact. "What do you mean?"

"Well, from what you said, there's no real proof that Marsh did this."

"Proof? Chris, we were just with the guy for two hours, remember? He did everything but pull a gun."

"Yeah, but I doubt that'll be good enough for the cops."

"Why not?"

"Look, if Marsh did it, he's smart enough to use gloves and all. There won't be any physical-type evidence at the scene."

I ground my teeth. "What about the divorce court, then?"

"It's like I said before about the court, John. It doesn't have any jurisdiction because we haven't filed anything yet."

"Which adds up to what?"

"Which adds up to there's no order of the court yet that Marsh violated. Assuming he did the cat."

"Jesus, Chris, you're the lawyer, not me. There must be something you can do about this."

"Well, I can call Felicia and put her on notice."

"Notice? Chris, the guy's a nut! Understand? Normal people don't do things like this. He's obviously trying to scare Hanna into giving in on the house. If he gets away with this, he'll just escalate till he gets everything."

"John, you—what?" I could hear Chris saying something off the telephone, then, "Jeez, John, I gotta get back to this closing here, the bank's attorney is gonna—"

"I don't give a rat's ass about the bank's attorney." I lowered my voice. "I'm sitting in an animal hospital with your client and her hysterical little girl who just saw her first pet flayed alive."

"All right, all right. I'll call Felicia right now. Just don't expect much, okay?"

He hung up. The receptionist looked at me with a sympathetic shrug. I apologized to her, and she said it didn't sound like it was my fault.

We waited for another forty minutes. I hadn't been in many places less conducive to passing the time comfortably. I asked the receptionist if I could use the phone again. This time the paging operator couldn't raise Chris. I depressed the cutoff button, called directory assistance, and tried the number they gave me.

"Law offices of Felicia Arnold. May I help you?"

"Let me speak to her, please."

"I'm sorry, Ms. Arnold is in conference. May I take—"

"Interrupt her and tell her that it's an emergency."

"May I ask what the nature—"

"Sure. The life of one of her clients, Roy Marsh, is at stake."

Hesitation. "Is this Mr. Marsh?"

"No. Now please get her on the phone."

I waited maybe thirty seconds before Arnold's voice said, "Mr. Cuddy?"

"Good guess."

"Mr. Cuddy, Chris Christides has already—"

"Look, Ms. Arnold. Let's cut the 'proper channels' bullshit, all right? I'm calling from an animal hospital

45

because your boy Marsh took a skinning knife to a kitten."

"I've already spoken to Roy, Mr. Cuddy. If you'd allow me to continue?"

"Go ahead."

"Mr. Marsh is shocked at the incident. He was at his home in Swampscott when I reached him, and he had driven directly there after our conference here."

"He have somebody backing him on that?"

"If you mean corroboration for what you evidently assume is an alibi, yes, yes he does."

"Who?"

"I'm not sure that's any of your—"

"Let me take a wild guess then. A certain nurse from Samaritan Hospital?"

"I can neither—"

"You really think she'll stand up? Credibly, I mean."

"Mr. Cuddy, you strike me as the sort of man who will do what you will. I can only advise you to seek independent counsel on your potential liability before you act."

"Liability for what? Malicious prosecution?"

She said, "Do call again when you can be a little more sociable," and hung up.

I handed the telephone back to the receptionist, who said, "Try counting to ten."

"There aren't enough numbers for this."

Just then the door to the back area opened and the veterinarian who had taken Cottontail came out. She pushed a hank of hair that looked stringy from sweat off her forehead and back behind her ear. She motioned to me without smiling as she crossed the room to where Hanna and Vickie, who now looked up, were sitting.

Hanna said, "Please . . . tell us?"

As I approached them, the vet hunkered down to Vickie's eye level on the bench. "Honey, I'm so sorry. But your kitty was just too little and lost too much blood."

Vickie responded with that Kabuki-mask slant that kids get to their eyes and mouth when they're about to shriek. Vickie whipped her face into her mother's breast and wailed, "She's dead, she's dead, she's dead . . . ," as Hanna, crying freely, said, "I'm so sorry, Vickie, I'm so sorry," then some phrases in German that I couldn't understand.

The vet straightened up and used the edge of an index finger to wipe a tear from her own cheek. In a subdued voice, she said to me, "Can I see you for a minute?"

We moved toward the desk and well away from Hanna and Vickie.

"My name's Mary Vesch."

"John Cuddy."

"You realize I have to report this?"

"Jesus, I should hope so."

"The police will want to know if there are any kids in the neighborhood who might have problems."

"I don't know, but I doubt that's it. I'm betting on her father."

"Her father? The little girl's, you mean?"

"Yes. He and the mother just split up, and this fits what I've seen of him."

Vesch huffed and shook her head. "I wish I hadn't given up smoking. I could really use a cigarette."

"Doctor, what happens now?"

"Mary, please." She looked past me toward Hanna and Vickie. "Probably not much."

"I'm sorry, Mary, but you're going to have to explain that one to me."

"I'll try. I report this as an obvious case of animal

47

abuse. If there was some kid on the block with a twisted streak, then maybe through the juvenile authorities we could do something, like therapy or at least counseling. But with . . ." She broke off and changed gears. "The father, I take it nobody saw him do it?"

"No indication yet that anybody even saw him in the area."

"And he'll be paying support, I suppose?"

"With his job, he can certainly afford to."

She shook her head again. "Then I can't see much happening to him. The maximum jail term under the statute is only a year, but the last time I remember a judge sentencing someone even to that, it was overturned on appeal. And here we've got a father that a judge isn't going to want branded with killing his little girl's pet and isn't going to put away because the guy can't work to pay support from a cell."

"So where does that leave us?"

"With a fine, but the most the law allows is only five hundred dollars." The errant ringlet of hair slid forward again, and she tucked it back into place. "Not much, huh?"

No, not much. And not nearly enough.

FIVE

As we drove back to Peabody, Hanna caressed Vickie, making reassuring noises about cat heaven. Vickie's crying became lower and thicker until she dropped off to sleep in her mother's arms. I asked Hanna about Vickie's seeing a doctor in case of insomnia or nightmares. Hanna said she would call a pediatrician to see if the child should have some medicine for sleeping.

Then I needed some further information.

"Hanna, I know this isn't going to be easy for you, but Chris mentioned that Roy had been seeing a nurse?"

She stopped stroking Vickie's hair and gazed out through the windshield. "Yes."

"From Samaritan Hospital?"

"Yes."

"Do you know her name?"

Hanna didn't reply for a minute. I didn't prod her. She said, "Sheilah Kelley."

49

"Can you describe her?"

"Tall, red hair, very red." Hanna looked out the side window. "Good figure, like me before Vickie."

"Do you know when she works there?"

"From four o'clock to midnight, I think."

I left it there, and we rode in silence the rest of the way.

The Seaway is one hell of a road for views. Driving north, first you see Swampscott harbor, then just open ocean. Finally, as the shoreline curves eastward, the jagged horizon of the Boston skyline rises ten miles south and west.

Number 13 was on the waterside of the street. The BMW 633i was black inside and out. It stood sleek and taut in the driveway closest to the garage doors. Behind it sat a little brown Toyota Tercel, nestled close but still blocking the sidewalk a bit. The Tercel had a Samaritan Hospital parking decal on its rear window.

I pulled fifty yards past the driveway, executed a three-point turn, and looked at my watch. Almost 3:15. I studied the house while I waited.

It was a tri-level contemporary, with a faked cupola and widow's walk at the third floor. The exterior sported cedar shake shingles and a deck on my side of the house that seemed to sweep around behind it and toward the ocean. I guessed it at four bedrooms, three baths, and way, way over the $150,000 appraisal. For my purposes, I especially liked the deck; they usually had sliding glass doors at the back leading into the living room.

At 3:25, a tall redheaded woman blew through the front doorway and hurried toward the Tercel. She wore nurses' whites and was fastening the two top buttons as she fumbled for her car keys. She jumped in, backed out, and sped off. I waited fifteen more minutes, then strolled over to the house.

The view from the deck ran the gamut from harbor to skyline. I didn't see the speed racer, but it probably was berthed at one of the clubs where Marsh had a membership. The deck boasted a gigantic gas grill, chichi lounge chairs, and art deco drink stands. Real class. The glass doors were there, too, just a little ajar. Even better.

I slipped into the living room, cool and dark with a cathedral ceiling. A deer's head was mounted high over the fireplace, crossed hunting rifles between it and the mantel. There were framed photographs of Marsh in various terrains, rifle butt resting pretentiously on a cocked hip and a dead animal's antlers being propped up unnaturally by various guides. The size of the creatures in the photos surprised me. I thought Roy was more the kind of guy who'd spend his summers clubbing baby seals.

A five-foot projection television screen such as you'd see in a proud sports bar dominated one corner of the room. Around it, I could see a lot of high-tech consoles on black-lacquered shelving. Both audio and video equipment, including a hand-held camera in an unlatched carrying case, a tripod, and at least three video-recorders. I didn't bother to look for the cassettes memorializing his favorite hunts.

When I got to the base of the staircase, I could hear stereo noise drifting down from the second floor, mixed with the sound of water running and drumming intermittently. My boy was taking a shower.

I climbed the steps carefully, not wanting vibration to give away what the hi-fi cooperatively covered. The water sound got louder as I entered the master bedroom suite. The sheets on the king-size bed were rumpled and dirty, a fresh, oval stain on them near the center of the mattress. The accordion louvers on the closets were arced outward, clothes tossed everywhere. The door to the master bath was open, probably to allow the music coming from the large speakers on customized stands in two corners of the bedroom to be heard. There was a forty-five-inch television screen in a third corner, with two more VCRs on shelves beneath it. I walked to the threshold and peered in.

Marsh was behind a frosted-glass shower door. I could make out his movements as he lathered and scrubbed himself. On the rung of the metal border was a large blue towel. I carefully tugged it off, then stepped back and underhanded it into the bedroom. I eased against a clothes hamper in the corner and waited.

Twenty seconds later, Marsh turned off the water, made a blubbering sound, and slid the door a third of the way on its track, fishing his hand out for the towel. He slapped perspiring glass a few times, and said, "Shit!" Then he yanked the door all the way open.

Naked he looked almost starved, about as much fat on him as you'd find in a stick of corn oil margarine. He had an armored division "Hell on Wheels" tattoo on one bicep and "Born to Kill" on the other. He saw me and jumped, losing his balance in the slippery tub and having to grab and somewhat dislocate the glass door to keep from falling. His genitalia shriveled up to nothing.

"What's the matter, mighty hunter, Sheilah wear you plumb out?"

He worked his mouth once, then caught his breath. "What the fuck do you—"

"I wanted to have a little talk with you. About your latest safari."

"What?"

"You know, to deepest, darkest Peabody."

Marsh started to come out of the shower, slinging his left leg over the tub wall and making a fist with his right hand. Before he could cock it, I took a quick step forward and jabbed with my index finger hard into the little half-moon hollow we all have just above the breastplate. That tends to scratch the windpipe and made Marsh clumsily step back, tripping on the tub wall and nearly falling again.

His voice croaked. "You . . . got . . . no right . . ."

"You're a funny guy to be talking about rights, pal. After what you did to your daughter's pet."

"I got . . . alibi . . ."

"You think old Sheilah's going to back you when she finds out what you did?"

"Get out."

"Not yet."

Marsh started to come forward again, then his brain took over and he stopped himself.

"You're learning, Marsh. And so far the tuition hasn't been too costly. Just a little sore throat."

"What do you . . . want?"

"I want you to behave yourself. I don't mean about the nurse and all. I mean you leave Hanna and Vickie alone, and leave the divorce stuff to the lawyers to work out."

His voice was returning, and Marsh regained a little vinegar along with it. "Or else what? You'll break my . . . writing hand, too?"

I walked up to him. He tried, God knows why, to slam the glass door shut in my face. I jammed it with the heel of my shoe, and the glass, unable to stand the torque and impact, shattered, big and little pieces falling down into and around the tub.

Marsh at least had the presence of mind to freeze. I put my hands in my pants pockets and shook them, making the fragments sift down off my legs and onto the floor.

Marsh looked at the bottom of the tub. He had only some small cuts with little springs of blood popping up on his feet and shins, but he was literally surrounded by splinters. "Jesus Christ, how am I supposed . . . to get out of here?"

I backed up. "Good question."

"Come on, man. You gotta get me some shoes . . . or something. I can't walk out of here in my bare feet."

"Take up your wounds with the nurse when she gets home."

"I'll get you for—"

"You've got a mighty short retention span, Marsh. Let me spell it out for you. Doing the cat today, you stepped outside the rules. You step outside the rules again, boyo, and I'll play like there are no rules. Understand?"

He didn't say anything until I was down the stairs. Then he started yelling, "Ow, ow! Goddamn fucking —Ow, ow—You son of a bitch—"

I left by the deck door and whistled on my way back to the Fiat. Just to avoid tempting fate, though, I started right up, made another three-point turn, and drove out the other end of the Seaway so as to avoid going past Natty Bumppo's front sights.

SIX
◆

"Jeez, John, Felicia Arnold is nipping at my balls over this."

Trying not to picture the metaphor, I put my feet up on the landlord's coffee table and cradled the phone receiver against my shoulder. "Chris—"

"You saw the kinda guy he is this morning. What the hell were you thinking of?"

"Chris, the kinda guy he is we call a sadist, get me? He tortured his little daughter's pet. Besides, I didn't do anything to him."

"Felicia says he was covered with cuts."

"Chris, as far as Felicia is concerned, I was never there."

"What?"

"I said as far as Felicia, or anybody else, is concerned, I was never at Marsh's house. I'll level with you, but deny it to anybody else."

"John, you broke in!"

"No, I didn't. The door to the deck was open, and I walked in."

"She says there was blood everywhere."

"The blood came from him slamming the glass shower door on my foot, Chris. I pushed him once, that's all, and no damage from that."

Chris stopped for a minute, then said, "How come this is just between you and me?"

"Because I don't like the idea of Marsh doing the cat and then being able to get away with denying it. He's somebody who doesn't believe things you just tell him. If I pay him a visit, then deny what I did too, maybe he'll get the idea that it's a two-way street, that if he can go into Hanna's place anytime he wants, I can do the same to him at his house. Active deterrence, you know?"

"Yeah, well, I just hope you haven't made matters worse."

"Speaking of making matters worse, what are we going to do about that second appraisal?"

"Just what I need right now."

"I saw it, Chris. The house, I mean. Have you?"

"No. Well, the photos from the appraisal there and all."

"It's a palace. The Vanderbilt mansion done up in hardwood."

"So?"

"So it's worth a fortune."

"Yeah, well, is it worth getting a nutcake like Marsh going again?"

"Also the insurance, Chris."

"The insurance?"

"Yeah, on the guy's life. If I were you, I'd check on that policy with the company that issued it."

visitors, I spotted Sheilah Kelley a few minutes later as she pushed a medicine cart toward the children's ward.

"Excuse me, Nurse Kelley?"

She lurched around, flagging already at the three-quarter point of her shift. Up close, I saw she had brown eyes and more freckles than pale skin around them.

"Can I help you with something?"

"My name's John Cuddy."

She stiffened and pursed her lips.

"Miss, you know who I am and why I'm here. Is there someplace we can talk privately?"

"Lemme see your badge."

"We're not allowed to carry one."

"What?"

"In Massachusetts, all we can carry is identification, no badge. Here."

She looked at it, buying time more than reading or checking anything. Then she turned away, shuttling the cart forward again. As I was about to speak, she said over her shoulder, "End of the corridor. There's a small playroom. I'll be with you in ten minutes."

I found it and went inside. The walls were done in early Bozo the Clown. Even stepping carefully, my shoes crunched the innumerable pieces of unnamable board games that lay scattered near a short-legged table. I gently swept a Barbie doll and a G.I. Joe from a Sesame Street floor cushion. Sitting down, I tried not to feel too foolish as I wondered whether Sheilah Kelley was calling Roy Marsh for guidance.

She came in just as I was about to get up to search for her. She leaned against the wall, staying near the door. "Five minutes."

"Why don't we skip the preliminaries, then. Tell me, did Roy actually have you hold the kitten down, or were you just the wheelman?"

She swallowed hard and tried not to blink. "Roy was with me all afternoon."

"In Swampscott."

"Right."

"In nursing school they must have made you cut into animals, anatomy class and all. Were the animals usually dead first, because Cottontail sure—"

"Stop it!"

She couldn't stop blinking now, and the tears came even as she brushed them away angrily.

I spoke more softly. "You work with kids. It's your job. How could you cover for the guy after what he did?"

She shivered and sank a little, then slid down the wall until her rump hit the floor. She used her arms to hug her knees, lowering her face into them like a sleeping sentry. "He was with me."

Time for a different tack. "How did you meet Marsh?"

She raised her head. "Why do you want to know?"

"Look, I'm not after you. You want to be loyal to Marsh, fine. The truth isn't going to bring back the cat or make Vickie feel any better. I just want to understand what happened so it won't happen again."

She said, "It won't," a little too quickly, then put her head back down.

I said as gently as I could, "You may love him, but you can't change him."

"Change him." She took a breath, then said, "I met him a few months ago. He drove himself in here, all beat up. I was covering in Emergency, and he was nice to me, sent me flowers for helping him. Then lunch, a drive to the beach. He . . ."

When she didn't continue, I said, "Ms. Kelley?"

She shook herself all over, like a dog just out of the water. "Look, Mr. Cuddy. I can't keep you from thinking what you want to think."

"No more than you can keep Roy from doing what he wants to do?"

"I said, nothing more's going to happen."

"How do you know? What if next time it's the wife?"

"Look, do you know . . . ? I'm twenty-nine years old, and I feel like ninety-nine. I work myself to sleep five nights a week here. Six years at this place, and I still get Mondays and Tuesdays off. How are you supposed to meet people that way? I know Roy has other girls. Plus, my father hates him, hates him for what he's doing to me. 'A married man, Sheilah, your mother, God rest her, we never taught you any better than that?'"

"What if next time it's the child, Sheilah?"

She scrunched her face, like a grotesquely older version of what Vickie had looked like at the vet's. "There's nothing I can do! I love him, can't you see that?"

Unfortunately, she looked so hopeless that I could. I got up and left her, head bobbing slightly as she cried.

I found a pay phone in the lobby and told the Bonham cop who answered that I wouldn't be at their firing range the next day. The scarecrow at the hospital security desk told me to forget the cafeteria and gave me directions to the nearest diner, where I bought eight Styrofoam cups of tea. I set the bag of cups on the passenger-side floor of the Fiat and drove to Peabody.

At the police station, I spoke briefly with the detective who had responded to the break-in earlier that evening. He said there wasn't much hope of anything official happening. Not exactly news.

I told him what I'd be doing that night, and he said, "It's your time, pal." Then he cleared me with the patrol supervisor in case anybody reported my car.

In the darkness, it took a while to find Hanna's house.

SEVEN

One thing that must be said for tea: When you're not used to drinking the stuff, the caffeine really keeps you awake. It also gives you the shakes and urges you to relieve yourself. Often. For the last symptom, the Styrofoam cups are reusable.

I sat and watched Hanna's place until my eyes glazed over. I perked up when somebody else's cat scooted into the shrubbery and came out a few seconds later, thrashing something in its mouth and proudly prancing in that successful stalker way. I lost track of him, but thirty minutes later he was back, nosing around the bushes again.

At fifteen past midnight, a car wandered down the street and jumped the curb at a driveway four houses away. A woman stumbled out, obviously drunk. She wore a dark dress that flashed purple in the car's courtesy light. A guy got out from behind the wheel, playfully fighting her for the front door key and almost forgetting to come back and close the driver-side door. They laughed and groped each other a little too frantically as they finally crossed the threshold.

A few hours later, I jumped when two birds zoomed by the windshield, so fast and so close they could have been a 3-D special effect. I couldn't remember anything but owls flying at night. Maybe the questing cat had spooked them.

An elderly lady in a bathrobe watched me from a third-floor window across the street. She was peering around a shade, but she had a hall light on somewhere behind her, producing a stark, clear silhouette. When I waved to her, she abruptly let the shade fall back. I expect she went to call the police.

At 3:10, the man who drove the purple dress home came hustling out of her house, trying to knot his tie, put on his jacket, and check his watch all at once. He hopped in, fishtailed out, and took off the way Sheilah Kelley had earlier that afternoon in Swampscott. Perhaps with equal reason for feeling guilty.

The rain began at 4:15, drops the size of dimes pelting the bugs on the windshield. I tried the wipers once, but I would have had to use them continuously to do much good, which would have been a bit conspicuous. I did my best to peer between the veins of water pulsing down the glass.

At 5:30, the showers abated, and the sky started to lighten. At 6:00 I saw a light go on in Hanna's apartment. Leaving the car, I disposed of the reused cups in a storm drain and creaked stiffly around the puddles to her door.

"You should not have stayed in a car all the night."

"I was afraid Roy might be back."

"On the telephone, you tell me he would not."

"I didn't want to chance being wrong."

Hanna set a glass of milk next to me. She reached over the counter and absently pulled a box of dry cat food from a cabinet. Shaking it like a dinner bell, she caught herself, said, "Oh," and put it in the trash.

She said, "At least you could knock on the door and come inside here."

"Roy was mad enough at you already. I didn't want him to think there was something else he should get even about."

She added milk to her coffee and joined me at the table. "Vickie is still asleep. From the doctor's pills."

When Hanna raised her eyes to me, I thought I saw a glimmer marked "invitation." I thought of the guy with the woman in the purple dress. I said, "How is Vickie doing?"

She sighed. "The same. She wakes up and she cries. A little less each time, maybe."

"Time will heal it."

"Yes. Time." She stirred her coffee unnecessarily. "Can I ask a question?"

"Sure."

"Chris said he would help me without any money."

"That doesn't sound like a question."

"I called two lawyers in Swampscott before I . . . left. They both say they would not talk to me without money."

"A retainer?"

"Yes. A retainer which I don't get back if I don't have them as my lawyer."

"And?"

"I don't want to be . . ." She stopped stirring, fixing me with an unhappy look. "John, do you think Chris is a good lawyer for me? And Vickie."

Uh-oh. "Why?"

"Yesterday. In the office with Roy and his lawyer. I

got . . . I think maybe Chris was not so willing to fight for me. Us."

"Hanna, I'm pretty ignorant about divorce. It does seem to me you ought to get a lot from Roy, but how much is right, or enough, I don't know."

"Yes." She went back to the coffee. "I'm sorry."

"There's nothing to be sorry about."

"Chris tries to help me for no money, and I worry he's no good. You try to help me for no money, and I try to make you tell me about Chris." She got up and ran tap water into her mug. "I'm sorry."

I floated out a change of subject. "Hanna, I think I know a faster way than time to cheer Vickie up."

She turned around, canting her head to the side.

"Oh, Mommie, she's so cute!"

Vickie was sitting on an aluminum folding chair, next to a honeycomb of cages, each one containing three or four kittens. The one on her lap had rolled over onto its back, writhing and purring in ecstasy as Vickie stroked its belly. Long hair of half a dozen colors, gene pool courtesy of Cuisinart. It was about as unlike Cottontail as it could be and still be called a cat.

Hanna kneeled down to scratch between its ears. Remembering Nancy's comment about an animal shelter in Salem, I had called the vet who'd helped us yesterday, and she'd given me the name and address.

The shelter volunteer we'd met at the door came over to us and said, "You're welcome to take any of the other kitties out of their cages, too."

Vickie lowered her torso protectively over the tiny animal. "No, no! This is the one."

The volunteer smiled. I said, "Looks like we've got a sale."

"The IRS says we have to call it a 'donation.' Why

66

don't you stay here while I finish with someone else at the desk? I'll just be a minute."

As she walked away, my eye was caught by a dog in one of the larger cages. He was some kind of terrier cross, maybe with a pointer. His legs were too long, his body too short, and he had a coarse, off-white coat with uneven orange blotches and scraggly whiskers. It was the look on his face that got me, though. A look that implied he knew he was an orphan, but not cute and cuddly, and therefore doomed to remain one. I turned away and hoped the volunteer would hurry.

I drove Hanna, Vickie, and replacement cat "Rocky" (don't even ask) home. Hanna insisted I stay for dinner, and through the kitchen window I watched Vickie play with her new pet in the small backyard. Nerida, Chris's former client who owned the building, came out and cooed and dangled a length of yarn that Rocky batted incessantly. Vickie was delighted.

"Thank you," said Hanna, cutting some vegetables into a steaming pot behind me.

"She's going to be all right."

"Soon."

Half an hour later, Hanna called Vickie for dinner, and the three of us sat down to family-recipe soup and bread. About midway through Hanna said, "You were in the army, John?"

"Yes."

"Overseas?"

"For a while."

"Germany?"

"No, Vietnam."

"Oh." She didn't say that it was too bad that Roy hadn't gone there and I to Germany, but she was thinking it.

After supper, I tried to reach Murphy but got no answer at his home number. I slept for about five hours on Hanna's couch. She tried to convince me to stay in the house this time, but I insisted on the car, calling the Peabody police to let them know I'd still be there.

By 11:30, I was back behind the wheel of the Fiat. Hanna had fixed me a thermos of tea with lemon, which I stood upright on the passenger's bucket. On the floor near the pedals was an old tin saucepan that she wordlessly had handed me on my way out the door.

Purple dress rolled in with a different guy, but he was too short to be Marsh in disguise. Aside from that diversion, Saturday night made Friday look like New Year's Eve.

EIGHT

I had Sunday lunch with Hanna and Vickie, Rocky mauling a catnipped cloth mouse in the corner of the kitchen. By then, I was fairly sure that Marsh had decided to take the hint I'd dropped at his house, and I left Peabody around 2:00 P.M.

Driving into Boston, I circled my block a few times to be sure old Roy hadn't decided to shift his aim to me. I parked behind my building and trudged up the stairs. I tried Nancy's number first, but apparently she wasn't back from New York yet. I reached Murphy's home, his wife calling to him to leave the grill alone for a while and come talk to me.

"Cuddy?"

"Hi, Lieutenant."

"We got company for barbecue, so I don't have too much time."

"Shoot."

"Your boy Marsh, Roy M., stirred some interest."

69

"How so?"

"Seems my friend in Narcotics has some photos of Marsh in the company of one J. J. Braxley."

"This Braxley a cocaine dealer?"

"Call him a distributor."

"Big-time?"

"Dawk—that's my narcotics man, Ned Dawkins— he didn't seem to think so. Braxley's a Crucian."

"As in Saint Croix?"

"Right. Come up from the island in the early seventies, set up shop. Not oversmart, but enough careful and enough lucky to stay out of the big shit so far. Probably deals with a white dude like your Marsh just to spread the snow line a little farther north without a whole lot of risk."

"Thanks, Lieutenant."

"Cuddy, you remember what I said to you. And don't you be messing with Braxley, either. Old J.J. like to use the muscle, and his hired help'd scare the Fridge off the football field."

"Good to know."

"I got a round of drinks to make here. Anything else?"

"Yeah. I've got to requalify at the range tomorrow. Can you put in a good word for me?"

I think he was laughing as he hung up.

The couch felt so good I figured I'd doze off for a while. I woke up at 9:15 P.M., hungry but still blurry after my two nights sitting upright. I heated some canned chili and put half of a frozen French baguette on top of the pot lid to defrost. I washed things down with a couple of Killian's Irish Red ales, tried Nancy again without success, and went to sleep in a real bed for a change.

* * *

70

To get to the Boston Police Revolver Range, you drive south on the Expressway to Neponset Circle, then over the bridge to Quincy Shore Drive. At a traffic light, you turn onto East Squantum Street, bearing left all the way and enjoying an unusual aspect of Dorchester Bay and the city behind it. You feel as though you're driving on a deserted causeway, winding toward some abandoned lighthouse. Then, just after several large water locks, you see the range compound, technically on a harbor chunk called Moon Island. I parked next to the one-story bungalow with the police department's blue-on-white sign.

Inside, the range officer took my name and told me to have a seat. He was about fifty-five, with curly gray hair and a soft-spoken manner. Handing me a duplicate of the instruction sheet you get at the licensing unit back at headquarters, he suggested I review it while he got some ammunition.

In Massachusetts, the right to carry a concealed firearm is governed by the police of the municipality in which you reside. You have to have reasonable grounds for needing a permit, and Boston's live-fire test involves shooting thirty rounds at various distances. All in the bull's eye would be a perfect 300. To pass, you need 210 points, a 70 percent score. Basically, that means hitting a roughly chest-size target with most of your thirty bullets. The problem is, if you shoot less than 210, you have to wait six months before you can try again.

The officer came back to me with an old tomato can in his hand. He took me out through a rear door, passing under the large-print sign that spelled out Boston Police Rule 303 ("The Use of Deadly Force is Permitted: . . . ."). We walked toward the numbered asphalt firing stations at the close edge of the range.

No one else was in sight. The blue target holders were posted about twenty-five yards away against a high reddish brown barrier and an even higher earth berm behind it.

The officer placed the can on the ground and unholstered his revolver. After checking to be sure the cylinder was empty, he stuck his fingers into and through the gun's frame to keep the cylinder swung out and safe. I slowly drew the four-inch Combat Masterpiece I had carried.

He said, "No, sir. You'll use my weapon. I'll be handing you the cartridges as appropriate. Please keep the barrel pointed downrange at all times and deposit the spent casings in the can."

I returned my piece to its holster and took his, keeping my fingers through the frame as he had.

"We'll move downrange now to the seven-yard line. You'll be firing twelve rounds from there."

We came to a stop at the target distance from which over half of the actual police gun battles are fought. "All six shots have to be fired one-handed, double-action. Do you understand what that means?"

"Yes."

"You can practice a few dry-fires with the weapon if you want."

"No, thanks." He doled out six bullets to me, and I loaded them.

"You may fire when ready."

I put my left hand in my pants pocket, assumed a bent-L arrangement with my feet, and took a deep breath, letting it out slowly. I inhaled again, aimed, and began to exhale, pulling the trigger without cocking the hammer. I repeated the procedure, including the deliberate breathing, five more times.

"Make it safe."

I swung the cylinder out, and we walked to the target.

He said, "Four tens, a nine, and an eight."

Back at the seven-yard line, I fired another string of six. Five tens and a nine.

As we moved to the fifteen-yard line, he said, "You have any prior experience?"

"With guns?"

"Uh-huh."

"Military Police. Mostly forty-fives."

He nodded.

"Weapon as finely balanced and maintained as yours would make anybody look better."

Another nod.

I fired my next three strings single-action, two-handed, with my feet spread wide and my shoulders and trunk hunched down in what's usually called the combat stance. My point total came to 289. We returned to the bungalow, and the officer certified my score in a logbook.

He handed me the necessary paperwork and shook my hand. "Hope we'll be seeing you again in five years, Mr. Cuddy."

I said thank you and decided it was the first time he'd actually smiled since I'd met him.

After the second ring, I heard, "Nancy Meagher."

"As a watchful taxpayer, I'd like to know why you're not guarding the common weal in court."

"Oh, hi, John. As a matter of fact, I should be, but after I broke my neck to catch the dawn shuttle back from La Guardia, the judge I'm trying before was in a fender bender this morning and still hasn't arrived."

"Will this screw up dinner tonight?"

"No way. Just drop by a little after six-thirty and see

the guard in the first-floor lobby. I'll come down as soon as he tells me you're here."

"See you then."

"Oh, John?"

"Yes?"

"Thanks for calling."

"Don't thank me. It's good to hear your voice."

"Bye, John."

I hung up the receiver and looked at my watch. Plenty of time for a quick lunch and a visit before going in to the office.

I'm glad about Nancy, John.

"Me, too. I think."

There's always going to be some uncertainty, you know.

"I know." I laid the baby tulips, mixed yellow and white, longways to her, just outside the shadow the marker threw.

You've seen enough of people who won't move forward with their lives.

I thought of what Roy was doing to Hanna and Vickie and said, "I'm working on a miserable case, kid. Divorce."

I thought you didn't do them.

"So did I. But it's a favor for Chris Christides."

Chris. Chris and Eleni.

"Right. She's no better, though. In fact, she's much worse. In a wheelchair now and so old, old and worn."

I squatted down beside the flowers. The topmost bud had opened a little, and the wind off the harbor bent the petals, like a moistened finger on the page of a book. "Remember how Chris used to revolve around her, spend all his time describing what new American thing she'd seen or learned?"

My mother used to say that.

74

"What?"

That you know you love people when you think of past times in terms of events in their lives rather than your own.

"I'm not sure Eleni and Chris qualify anymore."

Oh, I'm sorry.

"Yeah, me too."

I looked down the slope to the water. Two people with nothing better to do on a Monday than sail seemed to be racing each other as a low-slung, enormous freighter of some kind, black except for the rust patches, sloughed past them. The sailboats, probably twenty-five feet each, looked like tiny moths fluttering around a shambling old dog.

John, do you think Eleni is close?

She didn't have to say close to what. "I don't know much about MS. Just that it takes a long time to take you."

A minute passed, then: *If there's a time you think it would help, tell Eleni that afterwards isn't so bad.*

I backed and hauled, a half-turn of the wheel at a time, into the pitiful parking space in the alley behind my office building on Tremont Street. I could barely open the driver's door because of the Dempster Dumpster and the fringe of near-miss trash around it. In downtown Boston, however, a manageable slot for a car is nothing to get mad at. Plus, with the Fiat there, I could drive to the condo to shower and change before picking Nancy up for dinner.

I used the stairs to my office, which smelled musty when I unlocked the door and scooped up the mail. I left the door open and pulled up one of my windows, enjoying the bustle of the Common and letting the refreshing air cross-ventilate the room. I'd let slide two reports on insurance scams, so I wrote them out

75

longhand; the claims departments involved would have them typed and returned to me for signature.

After the reports, I read a letter request from a concerned mother in Kentucky. She believed that her Marbrey, aged fifteen, had run off to Boston and would get in more trouble than a rooster at a fox farm. Finding my name in a telephone directory at the library in Lexington, she trusted me because she once knew an honest storekeeper over to Clay City named Cuddy who came from back east somewheres. Enclosed was a weathered family photograph (with a penciled arrow pointing to a boy who couldn't have been older than ten) and a postal money order for $100. She didn't include a telephone number. I wrote her back a polite letter, returning the photo and the money order and suggesting that she contact me if she could assemble the laundry list of information I requested.

I called Hanna, who said that she'd seen no sign of Roy and that Vickie really loved her new kitty. I told her I thought the worst was over and that the divorce would probably go as smoothly as those things could.

I hung up, tried Chris's number, and got him on the third ring.

"Christides."

"Chris, John Cuddy."

"Jeez, what have you done now?"

"Nothing, Chris. That's why I was calling, to see if you needed anything else."

"Anything else? Listen, I got plenty now. A driving-under tomorrow morning with a guy whose Breathalyzer shoulda belonged to a beer vat, another closing with that bank—"

"Chris, Chris, nice and easy. Any progress on Hanna's case?"

"No, and if I don't have anything better to tell

Felicia Arnold than what you gave me on Friday, I don't see any."

"What do you mean?"

"Marsh is still saying you roughed him up."

"Believe me, I barely touched him. His wounds are self-inflicted."

"Yeah, well, you gotta remember that I'm telling Felicia—to cover your ass at your request, remember —that you weren't even there."

"That's right. Just like Marsh wasn't there at Hanna's house."

"Jeez, John, enough with the cat, all right? Anyway, Felicia says that while her client would have been, quote, 'reasonable and flexible,' your 'unprovoked attack' has changed all that."

"Chris, what are you saying?"

"I'm saying she's saying they're gonna litigate it now, understand me? No settlement, trial all the way."

And no easy ten thousand for Hanna's lawyer. "Chris, first of all you've got to see this for what it is."

"For what what is?"

"Felicia Arnold's 'let's litigate' talk. For God's sake, you said yourself you've got him on adultery."

"Yeah, but—"

"And I've got him even tighter."

"You do?"

"That's right."

"On what?"

I thought about whether I wanted Chris to know exactly what I had. "No details, yet. Just take my word for it. Marsh can't litigate this case. You push for the house, and they'll fold on it."

"Push for the house." He made a gargling noise. "John, do you have any idea how much paperwork I'll have to do on that? Jeez, I can get my client a quick

fifty-five, plus probably a car and enough furniture to
set up in a nice apartment, maybe—"

"Chris, your client doesn't want an apartment. She
wants the house, for her and Vickie, and I don't blame
her. Look," I said, stretching a point, "I told her you
were a tiger in these kinds of cases. You push the other
side, and push hard. They'll give in, hell, they'll beg
you to take the house and probably pay you twice the
fee they trotted out on Friday."

"Twice?"

"Guaranteed."

"I don't know."

"Trust me, Chris. They don't dare fight. And if they
keep giving you trouble, I'll call Marsh—"

"Jeez, John—"

"—I said I'd call him, and have a little talk with
him about stuff he doesn't want aired in court. No
more trouble unless he starts it."

The conversation wound down from there. Replacing the receiver, I tried not to think about the pulling
guard I'd known in college.

I worked for another hour or so, doing bills and the
assorted other trivia that had piled up. At 5:10, I
closed up and went downstairs. The rush hour crowd
was just filling Tremont as I walked around two
corners and into the little alley. My car was the only
one left. The building threw a deep shadow, and my
eyes were slow to adjust, as though I were plunging
into a tunnel on a sunny day. Digging into my pocket
for the car keys, I heard a little shuffling noise in the
ground trash next to the dumpster. I thought, "Rats, I
knew we'd get rats." Then something hit me just
behind my right ear and night fell somewhat early.

The sweet scent of Creamsicle. Actually, somewhat
turned Creamsicle. I started to sit up, but lost my

balance and banged my head on something metallic and heavy. A wave of nausea swept over me, and I rolled over instinctively. I threw up two good ones, then followed with some dry heaves as the complex stench of the surrounding air caught up with me and my other senses kicked in. My face and hands felt wet and sticky and the support under my palms and knees was uncertain, here sharp and unyielding, there soft and mushy.

I was lying in garbage.

I slowly braced my legs, got a good purchase with one arm, and strained until I got up. I was next to the dumpster, grabbing the lid and causing it to clang against some chain-restraint. It was twilight. I looked at my watch: 9:10. Shit, Nancy—wait a minute.

I still had my watch. I reached for my wallet. All there but the cash. My car and house keys still in the other pocket. Around the back—uh-oh. No gun. Cash and firearm. A mugger, but a pro.

The Fiat was still where I'd left it. I gingerly probed the back of my head and brought my hand around for inspection. Lots of refuse colors, but no bright red. If I'd been cut by whatever hit me, it was closed and dried.

Playing a couple of coordination games, I could make all my limbs work, and I was seeing only the right number of fingers. I drove the ten or so blocks home like a fastidious drunk, taking double the usual time to get there. Up in the apartment, I tried to call Nancy, but her line was busy. Twice.

I considered reporting the missing gun. Then I thought about the details the cop who answered would want. Chewing four aspirin, I decided tomorrow would be plenty of time.

As things turned out, it wasn't.

NINE

Ironically, I was awakened by a garbage truck clanking and grinding its way down the alley behind the condo. I had focused on calling Nancy when I heard the pounding at my front door. I got up, just dizzy enough to have to use both hands to guide me through the bedroom doorway.

"Who is it?"

"Murphy. Open up."

I unlocked the door. There was a youngish guy in a cheap suit standing behind Murphy. The young one eased his hand out from under his coat when he saw I couldn't be carrying. He had a ruddy complexion and that unformed, almost larval lack of features that some cops have.

Murphy said, "Cuddy, I ever ask you to do something without a reason?"

"Not that I know of."

"This is Detective Guinness. He works Homicide

with Lieutenant Holt's squad. They want to talk with you."

"What about?"

"Now, pal," said Guinness.

Murphy spoke to him without turning his head. "Guinness, I hear you talk one more time before I'm finished . . ."

"Sorry, Lieutenant."

"Why don't you two come in and sit down while I get dressed?"

I half expected Guinness to check my windows for a fire escape. I left the bedroom door open as they went into the living room. Putting on some comfortable clothes, I tried to think things through. I didn't like Murphy's being on edge. I especially didn't like his showing up with a cop from another lieutenant's squad.

Murphy was sitting on the couch, Guinness standing close to the front door, hands in pockets.

I said, "Now, what's this all about?"

Murphy said, "There's been a killing. They want to talk with you."

"Who was killed?"

Murphy addressed Guinness. "You listen to what I tell this man so Holt hears it the same from both of us." Then to me, "Roy Marsh ended up dead last night. With a hooker."

I shook my head.

Murphy said, "When Marsh's name came up, I told Holt that I checked around on the guy at your request. Including my talk with Ned Dawkins from Narcotics." Guinness seemed about to speak when Murphy said, "That's all I can tell you."

"Can I make a phone call first?"

"When we get there," said Guinness.

* * *

Murphy left us at the elevator. Guinness took me down the hall, slowing his pace near a couple of older guys who watched us from a bench. One wore thick glasses and seemed washed out and boozy. The other one had a black patch tied over one eye but appeared alert.

Guinness shunted me into an interrogation room. Green metal table, three chairs, no window. A tall, slim black lolled in one of the chairs. He was dressed in street clothes, as in living-on-the-street clothes.

Guinness said, "This is Sergeant Dawkins. He's gonna be present while we talk. Wait here till I get the lieutenant." Guinness closed the door behind him.

"John Cuddy," I said to Dawkins.

"No surprise there." He tipped his head back till the top ridge of the seat supported his neck, then let his arms hang limply.

A long two minutes later, Guinness swung open the door and held it for a shorter, thickset guy in his late forties. He had steel gray hair cropped so short that it seemed to be growing upward over his ears. "He had his rights?"

"In the car, Lieutenant."

Looking at me, the new arrival said, "My name's Holt." He laid a file folder on the table. Some documents were in it but there was no labeling on it. It appeared he wasn't going to wait for a stenographer. A good sign, meant to show me we were all just allies here, debriefing each other informally. Right.

Holt said, "I hear Murphy told you that Marsh and a hooker are dead."

"No."

"What?"

"I said, no. All Murphy told me was that Marsh was found dead with a hooker. Nothing about her being dead, too."

Holt squared his shoulders. "I'm tired, Cuddy. And I don't want any shit from you."

"You want anything from me, you better talk nicer."

Guinness came forward, Holt stopping him with a palm on the chest. Dawkins looked as bored as an usher at a long-running movie.

"Murphy says you're a wiseass but that you'll cooperate."

"Ask your questions."

"Where were you last night, seven to nine P.M.?"

"Sleeping against a Dempster Dumpster."

"What?"

I explained about the mugging.

Guinness said, "Who saw you?"

"Far as I know, nobody."

Holt said, "Let me get this straight. You leave your office at five-ten, when Tremont Street looks like fire drill time at the fucken anthill, and nobody sees you get hit?"

"Like I said, my car was parked around back, in the alley, in the shadows."

"The only car there when you got to it."

"Right."

"And this mugger was waiting for you."

"Right."

"Only one car there, the guy musta been waiting for you in particular."

"Maybe. Maybe just for the one person he could nail at that time of day without attracting attention."

"Why didn't you report the gun?"

"I told you, I was punchy, still a little sick. When I got home, I just fell into bed."

Guinness said, "You didn't go to the hospital."

"No."

"Or call a doctor."

"No."

"Why not?"

"I've been hit before. My coordination and all seemed okay."

Holt said, "Let's have a look at the head."

I touched my chin to my chest as he examined behind my ear. I jumped when he hit the spot.

Holt said, "Not much of a bruise."

"It did the trick."

"Pretty easy to whack yourself there, you know how."

"So?"

"So why should we think all this went down the way you say it did?"

"Look, you think I killed Marsh and the prostitute, right?"

"So far."

"Why?"

Holt said, "When we found out who Marsh was, we called his house. His girlfriend answered. Before she went nuts with the crying, we got his lawyer's name out of her."

"And Felicia Arnold told you Marsh and I didn't exactly hit it off at the divorce conference."

Guinness said, "She told us more—"

Holt cut him off. "It goes a little deeper than that, Cuddy." He fished in his folder, came out with a mug shot, and spun it by a corner over to me.

I looked down at it. Front and profile of an attractive, dark-haired woman in her late twenties. She was wearing a garish red-and-white-striped blouse and an exasperated expression.

Guinness said, "Know her?"

"No."

"Street name's Teri Angel. Pimp's name is Niño, but he says she was free-lancing last night."

"And Angel's the dead hooker?"

"Let's just say she was known to blow more than kisses."

"I still don't know her."

"You don't know her."

"No."

"She was found dead in the Barry Hotel."

The Barry was a run-down joint near South Station. "Their restaurant's really slipped the last few years."

"Yeah, only she didn't order nothing from room service. Shot, she was. Near naked."

"Dissatisfied customer?"

"We don't think so. Bellhop tells us Marsh was one of her regulars. Saw him coming in that night with a suitcase."

"Suitcase?"

"Uh-huh."

"Was Marsh done with the same gun?"

"No, he wasn't shot. He took a swan dive from the window."

"Didn't strike me as the suicide type."

"You tell us."

"Lieutenant, I wasn't there, all right? Any marks on him?"

Guinness laughed. "You kidding? The guy went through the glass on the twelfth floor. Somebody hits the ground from that high, if it wasn't wearing clothes, you wouldn't know it was human."

Holt said, "Except it wasn't."

"I don't get you."

"Marsh. He wasn't wearing clothes. Just bandages on his feet, briefs, and a pair of those latex stretch gloves."

"Lovely."

"Yeah. We figure him and the Angel were doing

beautiful things together when somebody interrupted them."

I said, "Look, Marsh came on like a piece of shit, but I wasn't about to kill him."

"Your gun, Cuddy."

"What?"

Guinness said, "Was your gun did the Angel."

"How do you know?"

"Registration number, you stupid shit. Computer matched you right off."

"You mean you found the gun at the scene?"

"On the floor, by the window. But we didn't find Marsh's clothes."

"His clothes."

"That's right. No clothes, his or the Angel's. And no suitcase."

I thought for a minute. "If he didn't have any clothes, how'd you ID him?"

Guinness said, "Thought you might wonder about that."

I turned back to Holt. "Lieutenant?"

"We found his wallet. On the floor in the closet, like maybe it fell out of his pants when they were hanging up."

"Before his pants pulled the disappearing act."

"Yeah."

Guinness said, "We also didn't find his stuff."

"What stuff?"

Holt said, "His cocaine stuff."

"That's where I come in," said Dawkins, speaking for only the second time. "Homicide here like to know why you killed Marsh and the fox. Me, I'd like to know what you did with a quarter-million street value of J. J. Braxley's snow."

I put my head down, taking a couple of deep breaths. "Somebody set me up."

Guinness said, "Sure they did."

"Think about it, will you? I get knocked out, they take my gun, kill Angel here and Marsh, and leave the weapon there to link me with a guy I already didn't like."

Holt said, "Or you fake the hit on the head, toss Marsh through the window, and lose the Angel as a witness."

"And leave my righteous gun at the scene?"

Holt and Guinness exchanged glances, Dawkins kept his eyes on me.

Holt said, "You don't have a righteous gun anymore, my friend."

"Meaning?"

"Meaning you didn't report the loss of your gun like you were supposed to, and the commissioner has pulled your license to carry."

"Just like that."

"The statute says he can do it 'for cause' and 'at his will.'"

"I told you why I didn't report it."

"The statute also says 'forthwith.' You lose it or get it stolen, you're supposed to report it 'forthwith,' not when you fucken get around to it."

Guinness said, "That means we catch you with a piece, you're gone for a year, pal. No deal, no parole, no way out."

I said, "Your theory is I do those things with a registered weapon instead of a throwaway, then leave the registered piece on the floor somewhere?"

Guinness said, "You got surprised, and—"

"I had a date scheduled with Nancy Meagher last night."

Holt said, "The assistant D.A.?"

"That's right. Because of getting hit, I stood her up. Tried to call her but never got through."

"You try to call her, but you're too punchy to report the gun, is that it?"

"That's it."

"So?"

"So your theory is I plan to ace Marsh, and do this Angel in the bargain, leave my traceable gun at the scene, then don't show up for a date with an assistant D.A. and don't even warn her."

"You panicked. Didn't think it through till this morning."

I jerked my head toward the door and immediately regretted it. Massaging behind my ear, I said, "And what about the little show-up outside there?"

"What show-up?"

"The two pensioners on the bench. The ones you brought in from the Barry. They live there or what?"

No response.

I said, "Either way, Lieutenant, they didn't make me, did they? You had a little talk after Guinness waltzed me past them, and neither one ever saw me before."

Guinness picked at his teeth. Holt and Dawkins just watched me.

"C'mon, Lieutenant. Somebody set me up, somebody who wanted Marsh dead."

Dawkins said, "Or the Angel."

Holt said to him, "The Angel?"

Dawkins said, "Yeah. Somebody wants the Angel dead, he just have to appreciate how Cuddy here have it in for Marsh." Dawkins treated me to a sugary smile. "'Course, I'd still like to know where J.J.'s stuff got to, and so will he."

Holt let me go, warning me to stay available and not to call Nancy until they had checked my story with her. I went up the hall and by the corner to Murphy's office. Nobody I recognized was around, so I walked up to his door and knocked.

"Yeah."

I entered, closing the door behind me.

Murphy looked up from a file he was reading. "Get out."

"Lieutenant, I wanted to thank you."

"I'm not supposed to be talking with you."

"You must have told Holt I wouldn't have done Marsh that stupidly. Otherwise, with what he had on my gun, he would have held me awhile."

"Cuddy, I will not talk with you about another squad's case. Now get out."

"This mean I can't get a look at the jacket on this?"

Murphy snapped the folder closed and came up out of his chair, shoulders hunched. "You fucking asshole! You did me a favor, fine, I do you one. Ask around on this guy Marsh. But then the guy turns up dead, and it smells so much like you I'm afraid to shit. Things develop, it does look too stupid for you, but how am I supposed to explain that to Holt, huh? Am I supposed to say, 'Nah, couldn't have been Cuddy, man. I seen Cuddy set up a killing, even covered him on it, and it was nothing like this'?"

"Lieutenant, I promised you something that time. I promised you I'd never do anything like that in your jurisdiction. Believe me, I didn't."

Murphy sank back down in his chair and reopened the file, trying to find his place. "Get out. I'm not gonna say it again."

TEN
◆

I hiked home to clear my head. Once there, I called Nancy's office, but the secretary said she was in court. I asked if Detective Guinness was there, and the secretary said, yes, would I like to speak with him? I told her no thanks and said I'd try again later.

Chris answered on the second ring.

"Chris, this is John Cuddy. I have to see you."

"Jeez, John, the cops already called me. I heard about Marsh on the late news."

"Can we talk if I get there in the next hour?"

"Oh, John, I'm up to my ears . . ."

"I'll be there by noontime, Chris. Don't go anywhere I can't find you." I hung up, cleaned up, and went down to the car.

I pushed open the door to Chris's waiting room. Sitting in one of the plastic chairs was a man with black wavy hair and a dark complexion. He wore a crudely cut suit with a narrow-collared white shirt and no tie. He watched me, collapsing a tissue-thin, crinkly newspaper with headlines in what looked like the Greek alphabet. As he was about to say something, Chris stuck his head out from the office.

"C'mon in, John. I hope this won't take too long. I'm really up to my—"

"It won't take long." I followed Chris into his office as the man in the chair followed me with his eyes.

"His name's Fotis. Eleni's cousin."

"He doesn't look too good for business, glaring in your reception area like that."

"What can I do, John? She's really rattled by this Marsh thing, not that I blame her. I'm in and out a lot, so she feels safer with Fotis and Nikos here for a while."

"Nikos another cousin?"

"Right. He's with Eleni. In the kitchen."

I didn't respond, so Chris said, "So, what can I do for you?"

I settled back in my chair. "You can explain why you didn't let on that Marsh was into the drug trade when you hired me."

Chris moved his tongue around against the inside of his cheek. "John, I didn't have any proof of that. Just the wife's say-so, for chrissake. I might have tried to use it if things went bad at the settlement conference, but the way we were going . . ."

"Chris, you asked me to bodyguard because you were afraid of the guy. It might have been nice for you to warn me about what you suspected instead of giving me that 'insurance salesman' line."

"John, I'm telling you, I didn't know for sure.

Christ, you'd think I'd been a customer of his or something."

"Were you?"

"Oh, John, c'mon . . ."

"Look, Chris, somebody set me up, understand? Somebody who knew enough about Marsh, and me, to see me as a good patsy. Now that isn't a whole lot of people."

"What do you mean, set up?"

I explained about the mugging and the cops' visit to my door. When I got to the gun, Chris said, "Holy shit."

"Now do you see what I mean?"

Chris kneaded his hands. "Jeez, John, I'm sorry. When the cops called, they didn't say anything about the gun." He looked away. "So somebody hits you and then plants your gun in the room. God in heaven."

"Chris, who knew about my blowup with Marsh at Felicia Arnold's office?"

"Aw, I don't know. Felicia, Hanna. I told Eleni a little bit about it."

"What about that guy in Arnold's office?"

"What guy?"

"I think his name was Paul Troller."

"Oh, he's . . . Look, I don't know him too well, you understand? But he isn't the first young stud lawyer Felicia's hired, if you get my drift."

"Any reason he'd have for doing Marsh?"

"Jeez, John, how would I know? Wait a minute. When did you say you got mugged?"

"Maybe five-fifteen, give or take a couple of minutes."

Chris shook his head. "No, that lets Troller out."

"Why?"

"The county bar association dinner was last night over in Salem, and they always do a cocktail thing

92

beforehand. Troller was on line, a couple people in front of me, ordering a drink."

"And what time was this?"

"No later than five-thirty. I remember thinking that if the bartender didn't speed things up, I'd never get another round in before dinner."

"What about Felicia?"

"Didn't see her. But I talked with her this morning, and I can't see how she could have anything to do with it."

"What did you talk about?"

"What do you think? Marsh's dying kinda screwed things up for me, you know."

"I don't follow."

Chris spread his hands on the desk. "Couple decides to get divorced, even if the papers are filed and everything, it isn't effective till it's final."

"Meaning?"

"Meaning Marsh's dying like that ends the divorce action."

"The law makes sense after all."

"You're not getting it. Hanna doesn't need me anymore."

"What about the settlement?"

"It's off. She doesn't need it now."

"Why not?"

Chris made a face. "Because she gets everything anyway. Felicia told me this morning Marsh was too fucking cheap to make a will, like to try to disinherit her. You can't really do that in this state, and some of it is gonna have to go into the kid's name, but basically everything goes to Hanna like she and Marsh were still lovey-dovey."

"Hanna gets the house?"

"Like I said. Everything."

I thought about somebody putting Marsh through

the window and shooting Teri Angel. Then I thought about Hanna's broad, sturdy body and her determination about the family hearth in Swampscott.

I looked up at Chris, but he was already standing and shrugging into a sports coat that hung very lopsided on him, as if there was a great weight in his pocket.

"John, I'm sorry, but I really got to get on the road here."

"What's in the coat?"

"Huh?"

"The pocket."

"Oh." He reached in, then withdrew his hand again. "I got a permit to keep one in the house a long time ago, back when Eleni first . . . got sick and couldn't move around so good. For burglars, you know? Now this thing's got Eleni so scared, with drugs and all being involved, that I just carry it around the place, make her feel better."

I tried to catch Chris's eyes. I'd have bet money he would scare before she would. But all he said as he brushed past me was "Hanna gets everything and I lose a ten-thousand-dollar fee. Jeez, if I went into the hat business, kids'd be born without heads, you know?"

When we walked back into the reception area, Fotis was standing, the paper folded and stuck in one of his jacket pockets. Something else weighed down the other pocket. The partisans' mountain stronghold.

Fotis said, "Eleni want to see you."

Chris stopped. "Hey, Fotis, I gotta get going here."

Fotis said, "Not you. Him."

Eleni and a not-quite-twin of Fotis were watching a game show on a nine-inch black-and-white in the kitchen. As I drew near, Eleni said, "Nikkie," and the twin reluctantly stood up, clicked off the set, and walked out of the room.

"Sit."

I rested my butt on a stool across from her. She said, "I told you that Marsh, he was a bad man."

"Eleni, somebody made it look like I killed him."

"Why somebody do that?"

"I don't know."

She let a wise smile crease the side of her face that didn't twitch. "I think different."

"What do you mean?"

"A bad man, that one. You saw what he done. His own child, a poor little animal. He deserve to die."

"And the girl?"

"A whore."

"They were still people."

Eleni's chin jutted forward defiantly. "A whore is a whore, and that man, he got what God would do."

"What do you mean?"

"I understand you, John. I know you. If you kill him, I understand."

"Eleni, I didn't."

She called out "Nikkie," then a few Greek words. She looked up to me with the smile again. "He got what God would do. Nobody should blame you."

I drove to Swampscott and spotted the STANSFIELD INSURANCE AGENCY sign centered over the doorway of a large white house on the main drag. I parked on the road and admired the condition of the exterior, down to the green shutters and brass hardware. It looked as if fanatic maintenance had prevented the need for extensive restoration.

Just inside the door was a waiting area covered with an intricate Oriental rug and proud captain's chairs, polished and positioned stiffly. It took a minute to register that the setting looked like one of those rooms in a museum that the public can view only through a sashed-off doorway, "A Typical Sitting Room of the Late Nineteenth Century."

"Can I, uh, help you?"

I turned around and saw a rangy, fortyish man in a button-down oxford shirt, wool Rooster tie, and twill slacks. He looked harried, with one of those long, almost horsey faces that you see in some of the North Shore towns, too many generations of inbreeding around the polo fields. He did exude a sort of raw-boned physical strength, the kind that would never look good but never go to fat, either.

"I'm sorry," I said. "I didn't see any receptionist, so I came on in."

"I'm afraid the agency is, uh, rather closed for the day. We've had a, uh, death in the firm."

"I know." There was a kid in my third-grade class who stammered. I extended a hand to try to help him feel at ease. "My name's John Cuddy."

We shook, his eyes blinking absently. "Cuddy, Cuddy? I'm sorry, but you're not, uh, one of our insureds, are you?"

"No, I'm not, Mr. . . ."

"Oh, sorry about that. Stansfield, uh, Bryce Stansfield's the name."

"I wonder if I could talk with you, Mr. Stansfield."

"I'm afraid—"

"It's about Roy."

"About Roy?"

"Yes. I'm a detective from Boston, and I'm looking into his murder."

"Uh, well, then." I expected him to ask for some identification. Instead he said, "Come in."

I followed him into a low-ceilinged office with a bay window looking onto the street from behind discreetly filtering curtains. His desk was covered with an avalanche of paperwork. I recognized some application forms moshed in with slim binders and bulkier policies. A word-processing station with a high-backed leather swivel chair dominated a wall where an executive credenza might otherwise rest. Stansfield swung the chair around to its designed position behind his desk and flipped a switch on the station, causing the monitor screen to sigh and implode the chartreuse-on-black lettering like the dying of a soul.

"Sorry for the clutter."

"Secretary on vacation?"

"No, actually I initiate most of the paperwork, and, uh, the absence of staff substantially improves the confidentiality of our work."

I shoveled my way past that and said, "I'd like to know if Marsh had any enemies you're aware of?"

"Enemies?"

"Yes."

He rubbed his chin with a bony index finger and thumb. "Well, no. No enemies."

"I'm told he made a lot of money through the agency here. That can sometimes lead to bad feelings."

"Roy's family situation had, uh, deteriorated rather badly recently. But he was an excellent insurance salesman. I don't believe I, uh, ever had a complaint about him."

"What about the other salesmen in the agency?"

"Others? There aren't any others."

"Just you and Marsh?"

"Yes. Well, uh, actually just Roy. He was sort of the outside, customer relations man. He was marvelous at that sort of thing. A lot like my, uh, uncle." Stansfield swung the chair and plucked an old photo in a stand-up frame from a table behind the desk. It showed a man in his fifties, with Stansfield's features but somehow stauncher, sharper. "My uncle Mark, Dad's oldest brother. Dad, uh, died in Korea, and Uncle Mark took me in. Raised me, especially after Mother passed on." The frame wavered in Stansfield's hand. "Uncle Mark, uh, built this agency from nothing in the forties. Of course"—Stansfield waved his free hand around as he replaced the frame on the table—"the family already had this, uh, house. The Stansfields were an old whaling family, and this was the mansion of Captain Josiah Stansfield who—"

"I wonder if we could get back to Roy Marsh?"

"Uh, yes. Sorry. When my uncle died, I . . . well, I was going through a, uh, divorce, and the agency was in need of a good outside chap, to meet the customers, renew old contacts, that sort of thing. Roy came along, and I was quite, uh, impressed with his enthusiasm."

"He got along well with your customers?"

"Yes. Well, uh, not all of them, of course. But that was hardly Roy's fault. Many of our customers had come to rely heavily on Uncle Mark and just couldn't, uh, imagine dealing with a newcomer. But Roy quickly made up for that, and more."

"How?"

"By establishing new business. You could hardly, uh, believe how successful he was in attracting clients. *I* could hardly believe it, and I'd already been in the business for umpty-ump years. And once he'd brought new clients into the fold, they were always, uh, increasing their coverage and adding riders." He moved his hand over the muddle on his desk. "Trust me, this is just the tip of the, uh, iceberg."

"So Marsh would beat the bushes and bring in the business, and then you'd execute the paperwork?"

"Well, uh, basically, yes. Our relationship is, uh, sorry, *was* amazingly symbiotic. You see, Roy didn't care that much for the technical side of the insurance game. Matching the right, uh, rider for the right peril and so on. That's my forte."

Most of which is done by the insuring company, anyway.

"I understand that Marsh maintained a pretty substantial life policy on himself."

"Uh, you do?"

I felt a little muscle in my stomach go "ping." "He represented during the divorce negotiations that he had a two-hundred-fifty-thousand-dollar face-amount policy in favor of his wife and daughter."

Stansfield looked uncomfortable. "Is the wife a, uh, suspect in his . . . death?"

"Mr. Stansfield, is there a policy or not?"

"Well, yes. And no."

"Maybe you'd better explain."

He looked around his desk for help, but didn't act as if he saw any. "Roy did have a policy on his life. Uh, in fact, two policies. One was what we call 'key man' insurance. Are you familiar with it?"

"Where a partnership or corporation takes out a policy on an important employee?"

"Correct."

"And there was such a policy on Marsh here?"

"Right. For, uh, two hundred fifty thousand."

"Payable . . ."

"Oh, to me. I mean, uh, the agency, technically, but Roy and I were so, uh, indispensable to each other, it's practically the same thing."

"And the other policy?"

"That's the problem, I'm afraid. You see, Roy is, uh, was such an impulsive fellow."

"Impulsive how?"

"Well, it was some months ago, I assume when things, uh, began to go sour at home, he came in one morning and told me to cancel the policy on him for, uh, his wife and child."

Great. "And?"

"And I tried to talk him out of it, of course. I, uh, told him I thought it irresponsible and that he certainly should sleep on it."

"What did he say?"

"He told me to go . . . uh, he told me it was none of my concern, and that the policy had best be canceled by that day, with a, uh, return to him of any unexpended premium, or else."

"Or else what?"

Stansfield made a noise that actually sounded like "ahem."

"Mr. Stansfield, or else what?"

"Roy didn't, uh, elaborate. He didn't have to. He could be quite . . . uh, imposing at times. Of course, I'm certain he wouldn't have . . ."

"Swung on you?"

Stansfield just slanted his head.

I said, "Any chance that the insurance could still be in effect?"

"For the beneficiaries to, uh, collect, you mean?"

"Yes."

"No. No, I'm afraid that is, uh, out of the question. I could give you the technical reasons if you need them for your, uh, report, but any grace period would have expired some time ago."

"Did you ever let Hanna know about the cancellation?"

"Hanna, his wife?"

"Right."

"No, I'm . . . uh, I didn't really know her that well, you see. We weren't, that is, Roy's and mine was really only a, uh, business relationship. We really didn't see each other socially."

No doubt. Unfortunately, though, that meant Hanna would have had no reason to believe that Roy's death wouldn't leave her and Vickie with $250,000.

"Let's get back to Roy's customers if we can."

"Certainly."

"Was there ever anything out of line about his claims ratios?"

"Uh, no, not at all. In fact, Roy's clients had very low claims rates."

"Any exceptions?"

"Exceptions?"

"Yes, any type of policy—casualty, theft, whatever —that seemed to have more than its share of losses?"

"Well, uh, certainly not that I noticed."

"How about any individual insureds?"

"No, not really. In fact, I often had so few calls that . . . uh, well, off the record?"

"Sure."

"Well, Roy chose his, uh, customers so carefully that some months, we had almost no claims to speak of. I mean, you'd, uh, almost have to wonder why a lot of these people were even *buying* insurance in the first place."

I thought I could guess.

ELEVEN

I had a quick lunch at a waterside clam shack and called my answering service from a pay phone. I had a message from somebody named Hector Rodríguez, who declined to leave his number but said he would call back. No message from Murphy, which I didn't find surprising. No message from Nancy either, which I did find disappointing. I hung up, got back in the car, and drove to Marblehead.

Felicia Arnold's receptionist smiled up at me. "Yes?"

"My name's John Cuddy. I was here last Friday."

"Yes?"

"I believe Ms. Arnold wants to see me."

"She didn't—"

"It's about Mr. Marsh. Roy Marsh."

"Oh." She seemed more confused than upset. "I'm sorry Ms. Arnold isn't available."

"Look, I'm not trying to make your job any harder than it has to be, but Mr. Marsh was murdered and I really think Ms. Arnold will want to talk to me. Can you call her somewhere?"

The receptionist started to say, "She said . . . ," then motioned me to a chair. "Please have a seat while I try to reach her."

She dialed too many numbers for an inside line, which relieved me. I had no desire to dance Paulie the Pugilist around the Kurdistan rug.

The receptionist hung up. She stood and beckoned me to her, then turned and led me ten steps toward the conference room. "Ms. Arnold wants to see you at home."

She pointed through the picture window to an understated but perfectly positioned villa across the harbor on Marblehead Neck. "It's that one."

I thought about the view Arnold's own office would have as well. "She can watch her house from here or her desk."

"She says it gives her something to work for." The woman suddenly blushed and asked me to excuse her.

There was a Mercedes sports coupe, top down, in the driveway. A fieldstone path led around to the back of the house and a large in-ground swimming pool. Felicia Arnold lay stretched out on one of two chaise lounges that had never sported a Zayre's price tag. She wore a European-style string bikini and Porsche sunglasses, which she tilted down ever so slightly as I approached her. On the cocktail table next to her was a portable telephone and two bottom-of-the-glass water rings.

"Mr. Cuddy. Good timing. The afternoon was just growing tiresome."

"Last night not enough for you?"

She slid the glasses back into place. "Was it for you?"

"Plenty." I sat down on the other chair. The surface was slick, sweaty. Up close, her legs appeared waxy smooth, no varicose veins or blemishes of any kind. She had striking muscle definition, even in her upper arms and shoulders. "The police said you directed them to me."

"My duty as an officer of the court."

"You don't seem too crushed by your client's death."

"Perhaps I'm not the sentimental type."

"Maybe—"

"What the hell do you want!"

I stood up and turned to the voice. Paul Troller, coming out of the house. He wore a leopardskin bikini bottom with a desk-job spare bulging over the front and a lot of baby oil catching the sunlight. Even so, I pegged him as a light heavyweight. There were two tall drinks in his hands, and a match for Arnold's sunglasses rode up above his hairline.

"I said—"

"I heard you, Paulie. This your house or hers?"

Troller thought about throwing the glasses, but instead set them down near the pool's edge, clinking them a little and sloshing some booze in his rage. He started to stride manfully over to us.

Arnold said, "Paul, I don't want any trouble."

"He has no right barging in here."

"He's not 'barging in,' Paul. I asked Mr. Cuddy to come over."

"You . . . asked him?"

"That's right. And I would like to confer with him privately now."

"Felicia, my God, he's wanted for a murder."

"Two murders," I said.

Troller's eyes seemed to have the same problem with light as Marsh's had. He looked at me as if he needed just one more little push.

Arnold saw it too. "Paul, please. Leave us alone."

Troller just about bit it back. "Give me your car keys."

"No."

He looked down at her, but behind the glasses I couldn't read her eyes.

"Felicia, you drove me over here, remember?"

"Like it was only an hour ago, Paul. It's a beautiful day. Why don't you jog home?"

She had the same control over her voice that she did over her body. I couldn't say the same for Troller, whose lips were as blue and shivering as a five-year-old's after a day in the surf. He turned and choked out, "See you tomorrow at the office," before stomping back into the house.

I sat down again. "You ever hear of the National Labor Relations Board?"

She smiled. "Paul's position isn't exactly unionized."

And my next line was supposed to be "And what exactly is Paul's position?" but instead I said, "You and Paulie there are among the few people who knew Marsh and I had mixed it up."

"And therefore?"

"Somebody who knew that set me up to look like his killer."

"Oh, John—"

"I prefer 'Mr. Cuddy.'"

She took her glasses all the way off and stared at me. "Why?"

"Maybe I'm not crazy about the way you treat people you call by their first names."

105

"You are a bit different, aren't you?"

"Let's talk about Marsh instead."

"Why bother? He's dead, so the divorce case is over."

"The murder case isn't."

"Oh, a lot of people could have known about you and Marsh. His girlfriend the nurse, his friends—"

"Assuming he had any—"

"—the police, Christides, Hanna . . ." Arnold stopped.

"Because Marsh had no will, Hanna gets everything, doesn't she?"

"Roy was rather stupid in a lot of ways, Mr. Cuddy."

"Tell me about them."

"Look, anyone who lives on the coast up here tends to hear stories."

"What kind of stories?"

"About fishermen whose insurance rates have gone so high they can't pay the premiums. But the banks that lent them the money to buy the boats won't let them leave the docks without full coverage. The real estate developers are bidding wharf space so high God herself couldn't keep up with it. So one night, one dark, rainy night, the lobsterman brings in a few bales instead of a few pots and clears in five hours what it'd take him five years to earn legitimately."

"Marsh wasn't exactly your overwhelmed fisherman."

"Everybody has pressure on them. Marsh gave me a handsome retainer, Mr. Cuddy. In cash. Drugs? I didn't ask. He would have settled, and I . . . Christides would have gotten Hanna a nice nest egg to start a new life. So instead you have to play El Cid with Roy, and he looks for love in at least one wrong place and ends up dead. Forever. If you just could

have waited till he was over the spouse-lock, nobody—"

"The spouse-lock?"

"Yes. It's a term some pop psychologists throw
around. It means being fixated on the spouse you're
about to lose, or already have lost through death or
divorce."

I couldn't avoid thinking about Beth as Arnold went
on.

"Roy didn't care about Hanna in the loving sense
anymore. Maybe he never did. But he wasn't about to
let her go. Not until he was finished with her. I was like
that with my husband. He died, out drinking with the
boys and killed in a car crash. I was twenty-one years
old. Fortunately we hadn't started a family yet, and I
damn well wasn't interested in starting one without
him. He had a whole-life policy that saw me through
law school without any debts. That way I could start
on my own, instead of for some potbellied lecher who
was the only lawyer interested in hiring a 'female
associate' back when I graduated. But I couldn't get
my husband off my mind for months afterwards, even
though it was his fault that I was alone and without
him."

I was still thinking about Beth when Arnold said,
"Are you all right?"

I said, "Yeah, fine."

"You look a bit weary. How about a drink?"

"No, thanks."

"Oh, come on. I'll bet we have a lot in common."

I looked at her a little too long. "No, I don't think
so." I stood to go.

"At least bring me the drinks that Paul made."

I walked toward the pool edge. She said, "You
know, Paul really couldn't have had anything to do
with 'setting you up,' as you say."

I thought about Chris giving him an alibi, but said, "And why's that?"

"Well, for one thing, he's too proud of his boxing prowess. If it had been him, he would have made sure you had seen him, so you'd know that *he* had beaten you."

I bent over and picked up the drinks. "Any other reason?"

"Yes. I litigated a lot of criminal cases before I gravitated to divorce practice. His attitude is all wrong. If he had done it, he already would have tasted his revenge and acted smug, not angry, toward you this afternoon."

I walked back, setting the glasses on her table.

She said, "I liked the way you handled yourself with Paul today."

"Macho posturing."

She laughed, deep in her throat the way some older women can. "Macho posturing can have its place. And charms."

Her left hand had been lying relaxed on her flat stomach. Now the fingertips slowly began strumming near her navel. The spider, mending a weak spot in the web.

"You know you ought to be more careful around Paulie, Ms. Arnold. There's no worse enemy than one you've trained yourself."

"Really?"

"While you think you're teaching him everything he knows, he's learning everything you know."

Her expression hardened. "Mr. Cuddy, I've kept myself looking like this and feeling fine by learning a lot myself. Over the years I watched plenty of women slide from bombshells into craters. I do aerobics and Nautilus three times a week, and I can recline-press as much as the average fifteen-year-old boy. When I need your advice, I'll ask for it."

I turned to go and went about ten steps before I said, "Oh, one more thing."

She'd pulled off half of one of the drinks already. "What is it?"

"How'd you happen to know Roy Marsh?"

"Oh," she said, thumb and index dipping toward the slice of lime in her drink and voice supremely casual, "He was my insurance agent."

From Marblehead I drove south, angling toward the Marsh house. I wanted to have a talk with Sheilah Kelley, and I remembered Chris mentioning she was off on Tuesdays. There was a car in the driveway, but it wasn't her little brown Toyota. The brightly polished red Buick was at least ten years old. I pulled to the curb three houses down and walked back up, ringing the bell in front this time.

A burly older man in a lumberjack's shirt yanked open the door. He had bushy eyebrows, a longish crew cut, and unfashionable muttonchop sideburns. He gave me a disgusted look and said, "We don't want any," as he swung the door closed.

I put my foot at the jamb and used the palm of my hand to cushion the door's arcing momentum. My greeter balled his right into a fist and was setting himself when I heard Nurse Sheilah's voice from inside call, "Who is it, Dad?"

He yelled to her but kept his attention on me. "Just some salesman who's gonna need new teeth."

I shifted my rear leg for balance and reached for my identification, saying, "Your daughter knows me, Mr. Kelley. I'm a private investigator."

Sheilah came up behind him. Her eyes were bleary,

her nose so red it looked windburned. She said, "What do you want now?"

Kelley wedged himself between her and me. "You're the guy the cops wanted. The one who killed Marsh and the hooker."

"Mr. Kelley, I didn't kill them. But I was involved, and I want to know why. Now we can stand here like this till the leaves turn, or we can talk quietly inside. Your choice."

Kelley wanted to try a punch, but his daughter slid her hand inside his free arm and then tightened her fingers over his bicep. "Dad, it'd be easier if we just let him in for a while."

"We got a lot of packing to do yet. I wanna be clear of here before the traffic starts."

"C'mon."

"I don't wanna be sitting on four ninety-five all day."

"Dad, please."

Kelley let go of the door and shook his daughter off as I came in and followed them down into the sunken living room. It looked disordered, but not as though somebody was packing. More like somebody had only half straightened things after a wild party.

Kelley stayed standing, ready to brawl. Sheilah crumpled into a chair. "Roy's dead. What can you possibly want with me now?"

I sat too, in order to appear less confrontational. "Ms. Kelley, I know you've been through a lot, and I haven't made it any easier so far. But somebody mugged me, then used my gun in the killings, and I intend to find out who."

"I don't know anything about that."

"Maybe if—"

"Sheilah said she don't know anything. My daughter says that, it's true."

110

"Maybe your daughter's a little scared."

Sheilah tensed, then tried to feign with a head shake. "I don't have anything to be scared of."

"The room looks ransacked. Were you here when they did it?"

"She already told you, she don't know anything. Why don't you just—"

"Dad, please." Sheilah raked her hair with her fingers. "Look, Mr. . . ."

"Cuddy, John Cuddy."

"Mr. Cuddy, Roy was into some bad stuff, with very bad people out of Boston."

"Sheil, for chrissake, you don't have to be—"

"Dad, stop! Please?"

Kelley glowered, folding his arms across his chest.

"Like I was saying, Roy was in with people. But I wasn't. I never had any part of it, and I sure don't want to be part of it now."

"Like it or not, Ms. Kelley, you are part of it. Or at least they think you are. Did they get what they came for?"

"How the hell would she know that?"

"Dad!" She turned back to me. "Mr. Cuddy, I don't know. I got here a few hours ago, and it was all torn apart. I ran out right away and called my dad from a pay phone. He drove down, and we came back in. I tried to pull things together again, so she . . . Roy's wife wouldn't think I've been trying to get away with something."

"She'd better not, or I'll—"

"Anyway, I can't see that anything's gone except the videotape things."

I looked around the room. The television and VCRs were still where I'd remembered seeing them. "You mean from the bedroom?"

"No, no. Not the playback stuff. The camera Roy

111

had. He was . . . crazy for the stuff. Camera case, tripod. All that's gone."

It didn't add up. A burglar should have taken all the portable, fenceable equipment. Even conceding a more particular searcher, why take the camera?

Kelley rocked a little, heel to toe. "Those all your questions?"

"No. Ms. Kelley, when was the last time you saw Roy?"

"She already told all this to the cops."

"I last, Jesus, I last saw him Sunday night, when I got home from work. We . . . went to sleep."

"You didn't see him yesterday morning?"

"No, I was still asleep. He was gone by the time I woke up."

"What else did you do yesterday?"

"It was my day off, you know? I got up, drove some errands and so on. I went—"

"Lookit, she had dinner with me last night at home. In Tullbury, awright? She wasn't anywhere near that hotel. She didn't have anything to do with it."

"Mr. Kelley, the cops said they called your daughter at this house."

"I was just in the door here when they called. Then I drove back to my dad's house."

"Why didn't you stay here?"

"I . . ." She stopped, resignedly reaching a decision. "All right, I *was* scared, okay? I knew the kind of people Roy was in with could have killed him, and I was scared they'd be around to see me."

"Did you know where Roy was going last night?"

Kelley uncrossed his arms. "The hell kind of question is that to ask?"

"Mr. Kelley, she was going to have dinner with you. That suggests that your daughter knew that Roy wasn't going to be here for dinner. That suggests—"

"If you're saying my daughter knew that bum was hanging around with a hooker, I'll bust your face like—"

"Dad!" The tears started to flow; she wiped her forearm across her face just once, violently, then turned to me. "Roy was a bastard. He two-timed his wife with me, and me with her . . . the prostitute. He didn't deserve all the things he had, but I loved him, mister, I loved him and I'm miserable he's gone."

"Honey, how—"

"Dad, shut up!"

"Sheilah, in front of—"

"Just please shut up!"

Kelley's face fell. He looked at me. "She's upset. She don't know what she's sayin'."

"Ms. Kelley?"

I could have poured a beer in the time it took her to say, "Yes?"

"The Boston police tell me Roy's connection is a pretty rough character. I think it'd be a good idea for you to stay out of sight for a while. Especially if they didn't find what they were looking for here."

"She's gonna stay with me. Back home in Tullbury. I was in the department twenny-seven years. Leo Kelley, Engine Company Number One. I got friends all over town. They can't touch her there."

Sheilah Kelley chewed on her lip. She didn't look too sure.

TWELVE

I detoured back to Peabody and found Hanna's street after only one wrong turn. The lights were on in her apartment as I walked up the path.

She pulled back the door, surprised to see me. "John Cuddy. You are all right?"

"Yes."

"The police, they said you were . . . hit?"

"Mugged. But I'm all right. Can I come in?"

"Oh, sure, sure." Hanna turned away. "Vickie is taking the nap now."

Since I couldn't see Hanna's face, I just said, "I'll be quiet."

I followed her into the living room and sat down across from her.

"The new kitten you got for Vickie, it is doing so much good."

"I'm glad. Hanna, the police have questioned you?"

"About the . . . Roy and the woman?"

"Yes."

"They come here this morning. They want to know about me."

"Where you were?"

"Yes. I was here with Vickie all the night."

"The police seem to accept that?"

"Yes. They say, 'Who can tell us this?' And I say, 'Nobody.' I did not see Nerida, and Vickie was asleep. But there is nothing I can do about that."

"Hanna, I've been to Roy's house."

"My house now."

"So Chris tells me. The nurse, the woman Roy was seeing, she's moving her things out."

Hanna sighed. "You know, I cannot blame her. Roy was, I don't know the English for it, but the women always like him. For the wrong reason."

"Some people are that way."

"Tell me. Do the women like you for the right reason?" She didn't smile at me, keeping her expression even and open, showing me assurance I don't think she felt.

"There's one in Boston who I hope does."

Hanna nodded, a little too vigorously. "That is good. That is the right way."

"Hanna, the house, your house in Swampscott, was searched by somebody."

"Burglars? I hear they watch the newspapers for the dead, then . . ."

"No. At least I don't think so. I think it was somebody looking for something."

"Money?"

I didn't answer her. She looked down and twisted her fingers. She said, "The drugs."

"Why didn't you tell me?"

"I told Chris. He was my lawyer. He didn't say to tell you. I thought you knew from Chris. I'm sorry."

"That's not the problem now. The problem now is that if Roy's playmates didn't find what they were looking for, they may think of other people to ask."

"I think I knew that something like this would happen to him. He was such a little boy about life. He really thought he could do anything and not be punished. . . ."

"The police think Roy had some drugs he was supposed to distribute. If you have any idea where they are . . ."

She almost laughed. "With the insurance from Roy, we have enough money now I don't have to sell the drugs."

"Hanna, there is no insurance."

I wanted to say it that way, directly and suddenly, to see her reaction. Her heart seemed to stop, but her eyes stayed steady. She swallowed and said, "No insurance?"

I told her what Stansfield told me.

She hung her head. "Such a little boy. My God, my God, I cannot pay to bury him."

I waited a moment, then said, "Hanna, I'm sorry, but I really have to know about the drugs."

She looked up, very tired. "I don't know to help you."

"Any idea at all where they'd be?"

"The nurse maybe. She might know better than me. When Roy and me were together, he used to carry them around in his case."

"His briefcase?"

"No. Roy had a lot of the . . . video things. He carried the drugs around in the case for the camera to fit in."

As I drove back into Boston, I tried to draw a profile of my mugger, at least by minimum physical requirements. Hanna had the strength to send Roy through the window, and a questionable alibi. Firefighters, even retired ones like Kelley, are strong as bulls, but Sheilah said her father was with her for dinner. Lawyer Paul had the muscle and sophistication, if not the inclination, to stage it, but Chris covered him. Felicia Arnold might have been able to force things with my gun, but Marsh would have tried to rush her rather than take a chance with a twelve-story drop. Maybe strength wasn't a factor at all. Whoever rapped me left me where I fell, and maybe Roy just tripped. So much for the process of elimination.

I took the Central Artery, skirting downtown on the harborside, and got off at South Station. I followed Summer Street into L Street to Nancy Meagher's address.

I rang her buzzer, the top one of the three-decker. I heard her coming down the stairs. When she recognized me, she said over her shoulder, "It's all right, Drew." The door to the second-floor apartment clicked shut.

"Still have Drew Lynch as house security?"

"Yes. You could have called first."

"I wanted you to be able to tell the cops I dropped in without warning."

She turned and started climbing the stairs. Maybe I should have said "without welcome" instead. I trailed behind her into the kitchen.

Nancy said, "Drink?"

"Yes. This remind you of anything?"

"What?"

"You and me. The last time you thought I'd done something wrong."

She paused with the glass she had taken down from the cabinet over the sink. "The last time I thought you'd done something wrong you'd killed a man."

"That was then. This time I was set up."

She pulled open the freezer door and plopped two ice cubes into the glass. "Pity the police don't agree with you."

"C'mon, Nancy—"

The glass crashed into the sink, shattering, as Nancy wheeled around. "Don't you dare! Don't you dare try to explain this away. We had a date, remember? You were coming by to pick me up. Well, I waited, and no call from the guard downstairs. So I tried your office. Nothing. Condo. Nothing. Then I waited some more. John's the kind who always shows, Nancy. The kind who always comes through."

"Nancy—"

"Then I thought, my God, he's had an accident. I tried the hospitals, Boston City, Mass General, even Beth Israel though it was the wrong direction. Then I got mad. Then I went home. Then I don't hear from you, I hear from a homicide cop—"

"They said not to call you."

"You were set up? I was set up, John! I was set up to be some kind of alibi you decided to discard." She put her hand to her mouth.

"Is that what you think?"

"That's what the cops think."

"Not my question."

Nancy said, "What happened?"

"Can we go into the living room? I don't need the drink."

"I do."

She built two cocktails and we carried them to the front of the apartment. She sat on the couch, legs and arms crossed. I took a floor cushion.

"No Renfield?"

"He's downstairs. Mrs. Lynch has taken a liking to him."

118

Nancy's tone said no more pleasantries. I told her everything I could think of about what had happened. Halfway through she uncrossed her legs. Near the end, she dropped her arms, too.

"John, why would somebody go through all that trouble to mark you as Marsh's killer?"

"I don't know. There are plenty of people who have pretty direct motives for wanting him dead. I assume I was just a convenient deflector for somebody."

She shook her head. "John, it doesn't make sense. The real killer should have been planning this kind of thing for months to pull it off right. You say you only met Marsh on Friday, three days before the murders."

"That's right."

"So how could anybody work that fast, take care of you so perfectly, then bungle the killings themselves, shooting only the woman and not both of them?"

"Nancy, I swear to you, I don't know."

"You don't even have a plausible theory. I can see why Holt and the boys wouldn't buy your story."

"That doesn't bother me. What would bother me is your not buying it."

She looked at me for a minute. "What does Murphy think?"

"He won't talk to me. I saw him after Holt questioned me, but there really isn't anything he can do. To use his words, how can he tell Holt I didn't stage things to kill Marsh when Murphy's way of knowing that is how much better I handled an earlier killing."

"Maybe I ought to call Murphy and commiserate with him."

"Is that a lawyer's way of admitting she believes me too?"

She set down her now empty glass. "You know something, John? I spend all day anticipating answers and revising questions to keep witnesses enough off balance that maybe they tell something close to the truth and not their convenient version of what happened. But I guess that has to be the difference here, doesn't it? I can't assume you're lying, because that would mean you set me up to alibi you and that would mean that everything I want to believe about you and me has gone up in smoke. On the other hand, your story makes so little sense that somebody as smart as you are would have done it better if he was trying to deceive anybody."

"So now the lawyer believes me?"

"No."

"No?"

"No. The lawyer believed you about halfway through. When you kept telling me what you thought happened without stopping to find out what I already told the police."

"For the lawyer that makes sense. But I have to know that Nancy believed me from the beginning, from when I just said I didn't do it."

She kneeled down next to me on the cushion. She hugged me and I hugged back.

Kissing me on the ear, she said, "You are the most aggravating man I have ever met," but I think she was smiling when she said it.

I left Nancy's a few minutes later. I was nearly to my parking space behind the condo when I realized I hadn't even thought of stopping to see Beth. At Nancy's, I was only a few blocks away, and it never occurred to me. No big thing, but . . .

I was still thinking about it when I got out of the car. There was a real stink coming from over by our trash cans. It was nearly dark, and I'd had about enough of garbage for a while. Then I heard the groaning.

Hurrying toward the cans, I started to gag from the

smell when I saw the feet, with shoes and socks still on, wiggle a bit. I bent down, covering my mouth and nose with my hand. A barrel-chested black man was lying on his back, eyes closed in a face like a clay mask formed by a clumsy child. Then he opened his eyes and smiled with both his remaining teeth. He brought a .45 from down the side of his leg up into my chest. Another black, tall and spiffily dressed, came out from the shadows leveling a chromed Colt Python with a six-inch barrel.

The second man spoke, his Caribbean accent thick and lilting. "Terdell, they tell us the mon was a true child of God."

Terdell said, "They right, J.J."

THIRTEEN

The Mercedes sedan rode smoothly over the potholes as Terdell guided us out of the city. I was sitting in the backseat with J.J., his Colt cocked and just out of lunging range.

Braxley wore a continental-cut, double-breasted suit, with a linen shirt, silk tie, and matching pocket hankie. His short hair converged to form the most pronounced widow's peak I'd ever seen, a Madison Avenue Dracula. A nasty scar began at the middle of his left cheek and arched elliptically back toward his left ear before trailing off at his jawline.

Unfortunately, I realized that the stench that made me gag at the trash cans came from Terdell. Even in the roomy car, his body odor was overwhelming.

I said, "Hey, Terdell, they ever make you file an environmental impact statement?"

J.J. laughed. Terdell swung his head around, his

features bloating into a smile, then turned back to watch the road.

J.J. said, "Mon, you think it bad now, you best pray Terdell, he don't fart till we in some fresh air."

Terdell chuckled, saying, "Which one you want me to hit him with?"

I said, "Which one?"

"Terdell, he name his farts, so I can pick one. His favorite is the Doctor J fart."

"The what?"

Terdell said, "The Doctor J fart. On account it hang in the air so long."

I said to J.J., "How do you stand him?"

"Terdell and me, we the perfect team, mon. The candy, it just about wipe out my sense of smell, and Terdell, he just can't help himself, that the way he is."

We were riding along Columbus Avenue, roughly paralleling the transit system's Southwest Corridor subway construction effort. "Where are we going?"

"Don't be too anxious to find out."

Terdell left Columbus and started using streets whose identifying signs were long gone. A couple of the blocks looked like news footage of West Beirut. The traffic around us began to lighten. After another ten minutes, I was pretty sure we were past the city limits. Then Terdell swerved onto a dirt road that had a lot of deep ruts, like heavy trucks make. After two hundred yards of bouncing and yawing, we pulled into a construction area and Terdell brought the Mercedes to a halt about twenty feet from a poorly lit drop-off.

Terdell got out, drew his weapon, and opened my door. I climbed out my side, J.J. out his.

J.J. looked around, smiled, and said, "Start walking," gesturing with his Colt in the direction of the slope.

I moved to the brink, stood sideways, and started down the incline in that hopping, stable way they teach you in basic training. My shoes immediately began to fill with dirt and pebbles. At the bottom of the slope I could see huge concrete pipes, six or eight feet in diameter, some connected with each other at forty-five or ninety-degree angles, some just lying separate, as though a giant's child had tired of the game. Terdell followed me down while J.J. drew a bead on me from up top. When Terdell could keep his gun steady on me again, J.J. came down. Careful and professional. Bad omens.

"Over there," said J.J.

We walked to an area near the apparent entrance to the pipe system. There were some makeshift benches, with broken tools, pieces of lumber, crushed tonic cans, and other debris lying around.

I glanced back at J.J. The car was out of sight behind the top of the slope. "I think Terdell forgot the picnic basket."

J.J. said, "Word on the street say you in good with the Boston police. Wouldn't do for us to have our talk where they got sway."

Terdell edged around to my right, still holding his gun.

I said to J.J., "What was it you wanted to talk about?"

"Mon, you can't figure that out, you in for a long evening."

Terdell kept moving, now just out of my peripheral vision. I heard him bending and scuffling with something on the ground. I pivoted, but Terdell was already swinging a five-foot section of two-by-four that caught me on the right side, belt high. I went down like the knight in *Ivanhoe* who's supposed to lose.

I inhaled deeply. No pain yet, just numbness on the side. I tested my right leg. It seemed to flex normally.

J.J. said, "You ready to talk with us now?"

"Ask your questions."

"Why you do my mon Marsh?"

"I didn't."

"Terdell."

I was up a half-count too slow, expecting Terdell to go for the home run stroke again. Instead, he used the wood the right way, jabbing like a riot baton into my solar plexus.

I fell backward, staring up at the night sky and making oomph noises while I tried to remember how to get the breathing muscles working again.

J.J. said, "Terdell, he can do this all night."

"All week," said Terdell.

"Now, why you ice my mon Marsh?"

"Set up . . . don't know who . . ."

J.J. shook his head. "Before I turn Terdell up another notch, let me explain to you what it is, slick. Marsh, he a piece of shit. He snort like a pig, and fuck like a goat. But he my piece of shit. And he have my stuff on him like two hours before he got the deads. I know, because I give it to him. And that means the dude who did him has my stuff now. And I want it."

"You want to . . . hear me out . . . or just raise blisters . . . on Babe Ruth here?"

J.J. uncocked the Colt and scratched his ear with the front sight. "Talk. I like what I hear, might be you get a break."

I levered up on one elbow, which seemed to open my lungs a little more. "I never met Marsh till Friday morning. . . . A lawyer I know asked me to bodyguard against him. . . ."

Terdell giggled and spit.

125

". . . Marsh killed his little girl's cat, and I called him on it. . . . I left him at his house on Friday afternoon, alive and well. . . . That's the last I ever saw of him."

"Street say your gun was in the hotel room."

"Somebody mugged me that afternoon. Took cash and the gun. . . . I was never in the hotel room and never even met . . . the girl he was with."

"I'm supposed to believe that?"

"If you're smart."

"Why?"

"Because if you're right, if I did kill Marsh and take the coke, I'd sure as hell . . . have planned it better and cleaner. And I would have had twenty-four hours to come up . . . with a better story than this."

Braxley slapped the barrel of the Colt lovingly in the palm of his off hand. "Mon, you know what that stuff worth, street value out in the 'burbs?"

"Where the users can get it without risking a drive into . . . the wrong parts of the city?"

"You got it. Two-fifty easy, maybe three, if Marsh know his customers and step on it different for each."

"Why is that your problem? . . . You can get another delivery boy up there, can't you?"

Braxley fumed. "It is my problem—shit, Terdell, hit this mon another one."

I wasn't near ready. I stumbled on the way up, and took a solid thump just at the tricep-shoulder intersection on the right side. It spun me around, with Terdell thrusting to my stomach as I squared up with him again. I dropped to all fours, quelling the shudders I felt starting inside me.

"Like I was saying, it is my problem because I give Marsh the credit. I ought to kill you now, letting you hear that, damage it would do to my reputation, word gets out. But Marsh, even with all his shit, he been steady for two, three years, which is a long time in this business, and the one time he step out of line, Terdell, he put Marsh in the hospital and Marsh, he learn his lesson. So when Marsh tell me he going through the divorce shit, and ask me for credit, I get the dumbs and let him have the stuff without the buy-money. Now I don't have the stuff, which I have paid for, and I don't have Marsh's buy-money. I have suppliers that expect me to take on more stuff next week, and I was counting on Marsh to pull me through." Braxley recocked the Colt and pointed it at me. "Now I'm counting on you."

"I don't have the stuff . . . and I don't know who does."

"You still got it wrong, mon. *I* don't have the stuff, and I expect you to get it for me."

"Somebody ransacked Marsh's house. . . ."

"Stuff wasn't there. Video case he carry it around in gone, too."

That didn't sound right. "What about the camera?"

"Terdell?"

I braced myself, but Terdell just talked. "I was looking for the case, but I don't remember seeing no camera, neither."

J.J. said, "Detective mon, you blowing smoke. That camera case was with Marsh when I seen him Monday before he got done. He put my stuff in it, like always. I didn't see no camera with him."

"What about a suitcase?"

"Suitcase?"

"Yeah. Cops said one of the hotel people . . . saw Marsh come in with a suitcase that night."

"They did, be the first time anybody ever check into the Barry with luggage." J.J. and Terdell laughed.

Then J.J. said, "Terdell, I'm going up to the car for a toot. Then we going to find out just how much more he know. Give this mon another tap, hold him while I'm gone."

Braxley holstered his piece while I tried to straighten up and parry. Terdell was already over me, this time using the wood just to push me onto my back. Then he put the end of the two-by-four squarely in the center of my chest and leaned into it. My breastbone bowed with the pressure, and I thought crazily about biology class and how the butterfly must feel when the needle is going in. Then Terdell eased off, suddenly driving the end of the wood to my jaw. I almost lost consciousness, and the stink from his being so close wasn't helping any.

I heard Braxley open and close the car door above us. Terdell said, "Honkie, you make it through this here, and somebody ask you what the closest you ever come to dying, you tell 'em about tonight, huh?"

Lifting my head was the best I could manage, but through the parade-rest space between Terdell's legs I saw a mirage. Or better, a hallucination. A short, skinny man shot out of the pipe mouth behind Terdell, approaching in silence despite his legs churning at insect speed. He held a snub-nosed revolver, and rapped the butt just to the rear of Terdell's right ear. The big man let out a breath, but no noise, sinking to his knees as he reflexively held onto the wood. The little man sapped him again, and Terdell fell flat forward, breaking his nose on the edge of the two-by-four that preceded him to the ground.

The little man whispered, "Can you walk?" His Spanish accent was so thick it came out, "Khan jew wok?"

I said, "With some help."

He got me up, tugged my arm around his shoulder, as if I had a leg wound, and hustled and dragged me into the concrete pipe. He shifted and adjusted my weight, and we hopped and scraped through the pipe, then took a junction to the right and one to the left, after which I stopped noticing or caring.

FOURTEEN

Dios mío, man, you a fucken mess."

The numbness from Terdell's stick work was melding into that throbbing pain that says it's bruised, but not broken. I rolled my head slowly and watched my savior drive. The lights we passed by and under flickered strobe-like over his face, which belonged on an olive-skinned twelve-year-old. He had short, kinky hair and delicate features, smudged here and there with grime and sweat. On his right hand near the knuckles were two homemade tattoos, faded blue crosses with the initials "H.R."

After we had wound through the maze of pipes, he had led me back out into the night, across a deserted road to his car. He'd helped me into the conservative white Oldsmobile 98, and I was dripping mostly mud and a little blood onto the white leather upholstery.

"I'm gonna be three days with the Armor-all, you know it?"

"Sorry. And thanks for getting me out of there."

"Oh, man, you with turdball Terdell for like an hour, was the only human thing to do."

"Mind me asking how you came to be in that pipe?"

"Long story, man. I call you office, but you not around, and I couldn't leave no number for you 'cause I was covering my territory, and I don't believe in no phone in the car like some fucken bloods think they exec-u-tives fooling the people watch them go by, you know? So, I stake out you house, wait for you, and I see J.J. and the Godzilla setting something up. I figure, lay chilly, see what happen. When they put the grab on you, I just follow along."

"I had a message from a Hector Rodríguez."

"That's me." He extended his hand. "But you ever got to find me on the street, you ask for Niño, huh?"

We shook. "You pimped for the dead girl."

He returned his hand to the wheel, frequently checking side and rearview mirrors. "Oh, harsh word, man. More like a broker. You gotta win the ladies' respect but let them keep some of it. No rough stuff, no dom-i-na-tion shit from me."

"You seemed to dominate Terdell pretty well back there."

"That was different. Coming out the pipes, it was like being back in the Nam." He looked at me, judging something. "You over there?"

We were winding down some of the same streets Terdell had used on the way in. "For a while."

"Thought so. You got the look. Who you with?"

"MPs. Mostly street patrol."

"Combat?"

"Some."

"You there for Tet?"

"Yeah."

"Bad shit."

"It was."

"I was before that. Iron Triangle with the Hundred Seventy-third Airborne. You a Cubano grunt and come in at five-five and maybe one twenty-five with ammo, they call you Niño and make you a tunnel rat. You ever go in one?"

"Not till tonight."

"Oh, walk in the park compared to the dinks' underground. They dig miles of tunnels, man, they fucken *lived* in the tunnels. It was like that movie, you know it? Science fiction thing with the foxy Yvette chick?"

"The Time Machine?"

"Yeah, yeah, it was like that. We was the beautiful people, the boo-coo beautiful American soldiers, man. But we was living on top of all these ugly dinks, digging their way to Saigon."

"Last I heard, they made it."

"Not while I was there, man." Niño warmed to it. "One of the bro's, he'd hear digging, see? It'd happen like that, you be taking five, next thing you know, it's like the fucken earth itching itself inside. The bro' would call me over, we wait it out, then punch through into the tunnel. We short on time, we just frag it. Took us months to see that didn't do no good. Fucken tunnels stronger than iron, man, after that gook gunk bake in the fucken sun."

He seemed to want to talk about it. "What if you had more time?"

"Oh, if we long on time and heavy on equipment, we blow some smoke into it, see what happens. We long on time, but short on equipment, I go in."

"With a forty-five?"

"Shit, no, man. Too much noise, fuck up you ears. I had a thirty-eight, some guys even go down to a twenty-two, but that was too fucken small for me."

132

"You wear a flak jacket or what?"

"Neg-a-tive. Too hot. You take off anything that clinks, leave you in the tee shirt, fatigue pants, and boots. Then you take the thirty-eight, a flashlight, and a stick. You tie the light to the stick with some commo wire or det cord, let you hold it out from you, trick the dink into shooting first where you ain't. Then you take the knife so you can feel around in front of you, find the booby traps before they find you."

I said without inflection, "Sounds great."

"Man, it was . . . it was like going back inside you mama, you know it? You move real slow, hands and knees, 'cause the dinks, they wasn't building no indoor tracks. The tunnels maybe a yard by a yard and a half, max, unless you got into one of the chambers."

"Chambers?"

"Yeah, you wouldn't believe it, you didn't see it. Some of the tunnels go down into dormitories, hospitals. I even heard some guys in the Big Red One found some kinda stage thing, like a theater, down one of their holes."

"How the hell did you keep track of where you were?"

"You fucken counted, man, counted and mem-orized like the teachers in second grade want you to, 'cause you forget how you come in, you ain't coming out next to your squad. You maybe coming out into some other outfit, who sees this little guy covered with dirt and sweat and shit. They see what looks like a dink coming out of a hole they didn't see a GI go into, they fucken open up on you, don't give you no chance to show 'em you speak the English with a nice Cubano edge on it."

"You actually see many enemy in the tunnels?"

"You don't see that much, man. Mostly you hear and you smell. *Madrón*, you think Terdell not nice to be near, you try some of the holes the dinks live in for months. I hit a tunnel had some rotten rice once, thought I was gonna die. Mostly you listen, though. You hear something, you stop everything, moving, sweating, breathing. Usually be some fucken animal, like a snake. Shit, you got so you could hear centipedes and spiders, it was so quiet and they was so big."

"And if it wasn't an animal?"

"Turns out to be a dink, man, you try to take him with the knife first, so maybe you get another one without the other one getting you. Sometimes it's a cold hole, no dinks, but you hit the jackpot, on weapons, medicals, all that good shit. Man, you think you a king, the king of the fucken tunnel rats. Other times you crawl three fucken miles and don't find nothing."

Niño stopped and took a breath. "Ain't talked about those days in a long fucken time."

"Some of them are hard to forget."

He looked over at me, confidingly, hands lying easy and capable on the wheel of the Olds. "You always be what you was then, you know it? You had the *cojones,* the balls, then, you got 'em now. You chickenshit then, you the same now."

"What did you want to talk with me about?"

"Huh?"

"When you called me. What did you want?"

"Oh, yeah, right. The Angel, she was a good worker, man. She free-lance a lot, but that's the way I run my ladies. Nobody got a slave collar on her."

"You the one introduced her to Marsh?"

"No. The ladies, they pick up the free-lance dudes on their own. She make me good money, though, and I looking for a little re-im-burse-ment."

"I didn't kill her. Or Marsh."

"Man, I believe it. I check you out. You so straight, the nuns take you back right now, no questions asked."

"So what's your angle?"

"Marsh have some of J.J.'s shit on him when he cooled. I could do some things with that stuff, move it somewhere it don't wreck no school kids while I make my profit."

"If I didn't kill Marsh, I don't know what happened to the cocaine."

"Yeah, but you per-sis-tent, man. Word is you a fucken bulldog."

"Meaning?"

"Meaning, I think you gonna find the stuff, but it might take a while, and I can't follow you 'round every day."

"So you get me away from Terdell and J.J., hoping I'll tell you if I find it before they do."

"Hey, man, I figure you owe me a favor for pulling you dick out of the fire." He took a card from his pocket and handed it to me. Just his name and a telephone number. "So maybe you pay me back with a little tip when the time come."

"To make up for you losing Angel."

"Fucken A."

"My friend, I'm not about to tip you about any drug stash. I'm just interested in finding out who killed Marsh and the Angel so I can get off the hook."

"Hey, so maybe I can help you there. You want to talk with some of my other ladies, maybe they can tell you things about the Angel."

I thought about it. Couldn't hurt. "When?"

"As they say in the Hollywood, let's do lunch."

"Jesus."

"Tomorrow. Say late, 'round one-thirty."

"Okay. Where?"

"I got a favorite place. La Flor. On Sommer off Appleton."

"South End?"

"You got it." Niño looked at me again. "You talk with her girlfriend yet?"

"Girlfriend?"

"The Angel, she like to see all the life can offer, man. She have this butch chick, name of Goldberg, Reena Goldberg."

"How do I find her?"

"South End. Just a coupla blocks from La Flor. She in the book."

"Thanks."

Niño scratched under his chin. "You didn't know about the girlfriend, you ain't seen the Angel's place yet either."

"That's right. The cops aren't exactly sharing notes with me."

He started to say something else, then stopped and said, "I got a key. To her apartment. You wanna see it?"

"Yeah."

"Tomorrow night, maybe. We talk about it at lunch."

He pulled up two blocks from my building, saying, "Sorry about the service, but if J.J. watching you place again, I don't want Terdell making me as the one who put him down."

"Your secret's safe. And thanks."

I got out of the car gingerly, then left my door open. "You looked pretty professional, sapping Terdell tonight."

"Man, you small as me, you gotta learn how to stop guys like him. Without killing them, I mean."

"Mind telling me where you were when I got hit Monday afternoon?"

136

He laughed and nailed the gas, using his acceleration to close the door as he moved out.

I walked toward the condominium building slowly, partly because of my aching body and partly because of watching for J.J. and Terdell. Aside from a couple walking hand in hand, I didn't see anybody.

When I reached the front stoop, a shadow began to move in the shrubbery. I registered a black face and started before I recognized him.

"Sergeant," I said.

Dawkins nodded. "You looking a little ragged, Cuddy."

I brushed at some of the mud, now caking dry here and there. "Want to come up?"

"That's what I'm here for."

He climbed the outside and inside stairs behind me, waiting patiently as I fumbled with the keys at each door. I motioned him into the living room. "I'm going to change before I sit on my landlord's furniture. Help yourself to the refrigerator if you want."

I went into the bedroom and eased out of the clothes I was wearing. I found some loose-fitting sweats and carried them into the bathroom.

I had a purple bruise swirled with red at each place where Terdell pasted me with the two-by-four. The skin under my chin from his last shot was broken, but closing over already in that regenerating, reassuring way skin has. I killed the light and went into the living room.

Dawkins was sitting back in a deep, comfortable chair, legs stretched out straight, arms spread-eagled, with a bottle of Molson's in his right hand. He was wearing a silk dress shirt and silk suit, sleeves pushed up to his elbows.

I sat on the couch, leaned back, and closed my eyes.

After about two minutes, Dawkins said, "Murphy said you a cool one."

"Look, it's been a long day, and I hurt like hell. What do you want?"

"Picked up a ripple that J.J. and his man Terdell out to talk with a guy tonight. Looks like you not their idea of good conversation."

"Word travels fast."

"Like the wind, babe. Like the wind."

"Just get to it, okay?"

"Okay. Marsh's stuff hasn't hit the street yet."

"How do you know?"

"J.J. deals in smallish quantity, but high quality. If shit that good appeared in somebody else's merchandise, I'd know about it."

"Couldn't a big dealer kind of hide it in his volume?"

"Yeah, and if he stepped on it enough times, nobody'd know the difference. But a major player ain't likely to deal with whoever did Marsh."

"Couldn't a major player have taken out Marsh himself?"

"Not the way it was done. Just be three holes in the head behind a building somewheres. No need to send him through the window and mess things up with the Angel."

"You said a major player wouldn't have dealt with the killer. Why?"

"Too much risk and no need. The big guys, they have import and distribution networks make Toyota go green with envy. Besides, if it did go down that way, we don't hear about it, 'less we bust the player with some goods, and the player roll over and give us the hitter to go easy on the drug charge."

"So where does that leave you?"

"Pawing the ground. A minor player, he'd have a hard time sitting on the stuff, follow?"

"Not exactly."

"Small fry does Marsh and the Angel, he must have need of money real bad. Maybe 'cause of a rip-off, maybe partial to the dog races and into a shy', whatever. Little guy can't afford to just sit on the stuff. He'd have to move it, or at least put out some feelers to the other small ones, who are sniffing around for the stuff anyway."

"And nobody's smelled anything."

"Right."

I stopped for a minute, thinking.

Dawkins said, "Now I bet you wondering why I been so forthcoming here tonight."

"After our session with Holt, that's exactly what I was wondering."

"Holt don't know about this little visit. And he ain't gonna."

"Because you're not going to tell him and I'm not going to tell him."

"That's right. This little visit is my own idea. I understand from Murphy that you just done him a favor."

"More like a return favor."

"Don't matter. He thought he trusted you, now he not so sure."

"I don't see Murphy sending me messages through you."

"He ain't. Like I said, I'm here on my own." Dawkins came forward, setting his now empty bottle down deliberately. "Now you listen up. You ask Murphy to run a guy down. He runs him down with me. Then the guy turns up dead, your gun at the scene. You got a fairy tale for it stinks worse than Terdell's asshole, and all of a sudden some white cops at our level start slipping the word to some white cops above us that maybe the Murphy and the Dawkins pulling something cute."

I thought about it. "Especially when Dawkins, the narc who knows everybody, can't account for why Marsh's goods haven't hit the street yet."

Dawkins barely moved his head up and down. "You think you smart, Cuddy. I hope to God you smart enough to follow this. Murphy got to be a lieutenant by being smart and straight. I made sergeant by just being smart. Him and me draw good salaries, benefits, I even got this next weekend off. We got too much into the department to get shoved into the shit by whatever it is you think you're doing."

"Meaning?"

"Meaning you got a file on you now, boy. File marked 'Narcotics.' You fuck up the Murphy and me in this, we may be out of the department, but before I go, I see to it that you found with dealer-weight snow in your absolute possession and control. And then you a long time gone to Walpole."

"I thought the Corrections Department called it 'Cedar Junction' now."

"A rose by any other name, babe." Dawkins stood and walked to the door. "There's something real hinky here. If you straight, you just might find Marsh's stuff yourself. That happens, I'd best be the first man you call."

He closed the door behind him. I thought about J.J., Niño, and now Dawkins. If I ever did find Marsh's stuff, I'd better have a roll of dimes on me for the phone.

FIFTEEN

After Dawkins left, I marched ice over the bruised areas, then went to bed. I slept until nearly nine the next morning, the hours washing away some of the pain but replacing it two for one with stiffness. I tried to limber up a little, running or any other real exercise being out of the question. I found Reena Goldberg in the White Pages. Her street in the South End was walking distance from me, but I remembered the block as being nothing but abandoned, burned-out factories and warehouses. I dialed her number.

After five rings, a strong female voice said, "Hello?"

"Reena Goldberg?"

"Yes?"

"Ms. Goldberg, I'm investigating the death of Roy Marsh and—"

"Oh, please! I've already told you guys everything I know. Twice."

Riding the cops' coattails, I said, "I'll be over to you

in an hour. Unless this afternoon would be easier for you?"

She exhaled loudly. "All right. An hour. You know the address." She hung up before I could ask her what apartment number, but you can't have everything.

I chose a short-sleeved sports shirt and some running pants with pockets and elastic waist to spare the need for a belt. For ten minutes, I watched out my windows, front and side. My car looked the way I left it, and I couldn't see anyone I didn't want to meet. I hobbled down the stairs and out the door.

After three blocks, the walking began to loosen up my injured parts. I felt nearly good by the time I hit Copley Place, an extravagant hotel-shopping mall complex that helps demarcate established Back Bay from the transitional South End. Just inside the Westin Hotel entrance is a magnificent fountain area, with contrived twin waterfalls that delicately and perpetually drop shimmering walls of wetness into the retaining pool below. As I got on the escalator that splits the waterfalls, I saw a man with torn, rolled-up pants carefully place the last layer of stained outerwear on the edge of the pool. He waded in, scooping up the coins that the tourists had tossed in, presumably while making their own wishes.

A middle-aged woman in designer clothes was standing in front of me on the escalator. Watching the man and wagging her head, she said, "Can you imagine anyone actually *doing* that?"

I said, "Maybe he hasn't eaten for a while."

She looked at me as though I'd just accused Ronald Reagan of pedophilia, then turned away and clumped up the steps until she reached the backs of the next highest bunch of people. By the time I reached the top, a security staffer in a golf blazer was calling for backup on a walkie-talkie, and I wasn't feeling so good anymore.

Goldberg's block stood basically as I remembered it, though less of it was actually standing since the last time I was there. Her address was a gray brick building with a veneered steel front door someone had tried peeling back without success. Ignoring an old, jammed buzzer, I pushed a bright nickel one. I waited two minutes, then pushed it again. There was a clanking noise, then the door opened. The woman behind it was perspiring and she said, "Don't be so impatient. I had to come down from the loft, you know."

"If I hadn't called first, how would you have known who it was?"

"If you hadn't called first, I wouldn't have come to the door at all. You want to talk down here or upstairs?"

"Down here" looked like a bombed-out German aircraft plant. "Let's try upstairs."

She secured things behind me, including a bolt like the one the natives used to keep King Kong on his side of the wall. "Come on then."

We went up a central, industrial-strength spiral staircase for the equivalent of four floors, then through a sealable trapdoor into her loft. The windows, or more accurately, the skylights, angled sixty degrees away from the roof, bathing the huge studio with sunshine. There were a dozen pieces of hewn furniture, in varying stages of completion, scattered around the room. She seemed to specialize in hardwood kitchen and bath cabinets.

Goldberg walked toward a thickly upholstered but gut-sprung armchair that was obscured by a nearly finished floor cabinet that must have weighed fifty pounds. She bent over and hoisted the cabinet to chest level.

"Can I give you a hand with that?"

"I can manage." She moved it off to the side without apparent effort and then flopped into the chair. Pushing forty if not past it, she was wearing a plaid shirt with the sleeves unbuttoned and old army camouflage pants. Both were as covered with sawdust as the floor around her. Her hair was short, parted in the center and combed to the sides like an 1890s judge. She said, "Homicide or Narcotics?"

"Neither. My name's John Cuddy. I'm the guy the cops thought was the killer."

Tugging on an earlobe with her left hand, Goldberg slid her hand down the chair's fanny cushion. She came up with a survivalist knife about a foot long. "You have another gun, I'm dead. You don't, you are."

I lowered my rump onto the third rung of a ladder beyond threatening range. "Nice trick, but if you think somebody's going to try to take you, it's usually better not to be caught sitting down."

"What do you want?"

"Somebody set me up for the killing. Mugged me beforehand, took my gun and used it. I want to find out who and why."

"The cops still think it was you?"

"Reasonable people seem to differ on that."

She laughed, but the knife didn't waver. "Like I told you on the phone, I already talked to the cops. Both Homicide and a black guy from Narcotics. They didn't seem to think I knew anything that mattered."

"Mind answering a few questions for me anyway?"

She brought the knife down to her lap. "Go ahead," without enthusiasm.

144

"I already talked with a man called Niño. His real name is—"

"I know who he is."

"He's arranging for me to talk with some of Teri's . . ." I stopped.

"What's the matter, you can't say the words? I can. Some of her 'hooker friends,' you mean."

"It's not that. I just realized. All the police and Niño ever told me was her street name. I never heard them use her real name."

Goldberg bit her lower lip. She looked down at the knife and said, "They never bothered to. Not even the cops when they were talking with me. Always just 'the Angel,' like she was some kind of car model you referred to like that."

I waited. She finally looked up and said quietly, "It was Teri, actually. Or Theresa. Theresa Papangelis. That's where she got the Angel part from."

"Tomorrow I'll be seeing some of the other women she knew through Niño. Can you tell me something about her they won't?"

"I don't know. We met at . . . this bar for women. Meeting is easier now than when I was younger. Back in high school my mother was always pointing me toward guys, especially the smart ones. But it's kind of hard to care about the president of the biology club when you have your eye on the captain of the cheerleaders, you know?"

"How long ago did you meet her?"

"About a year. When Teri walked in that night, she was spectacular. Every head in the place turned to watch her. She came right over to me and sat down and said, 'You have kind eyes.' Just like that. We came home here, and I'd see her maybe every two weeks or so."

She stopped, so I said, "Did she talk much about her life?"

"No. Not if you mean 'the life.' I didn't even know . . . No, that's not fair. She didn't tell me for a month or so, but I guessed it from her clothes and the fact she would come to see me but I couldn't come to see her. At first, I thought maybe she was married, but then she finally told me, and I wasn't surprised."

"Was she thinking about leaving it? Prostitution, I mean."

"Not that she ever said. Just that . . ."

"Yes?"

Goldberg flapped her hand. "Just that she had this dream of becoming an actress. That she thought the life had taught her enough about how to act different than she felt, and that she thought that was better training for the movies than some drama school she'd gotten mail about."

"She ever pursue the acting idea?"

"Not that I know of."

"Niño told me that she was . . . wasn't involved in anything he'd arranged for the night she was killed. Does that sound consistent to you?"

"Yeah. You were going to say she was 'free-lancing,' weren't you?"

"Yes."

"Thanks for trying to spare my feelings, but I did know she was a whore, you know?"

"I know."

"I mean, whether she arranged it or Niño arranged it never changed what she was doing, did it?"

"I guess not."

Goldberg toned down a bit. "She free-lanced a lot. I don't think Niño really cared about that. He's not exactly your stereotypical pimp."

"Is that how she met Marsh?"

"I don't know. I know she was really proud that she wasn't just a party girl Niño set up with conventioneers. I think she . . . I think she had trouble with the law before she met Niño, and I think she liked the fact that her personal clients now were in banking and insurance and so on. Like it gave her status."

"Ms. Goldb—"

"Reena, please. Don't you think by this point you could call me Reena?"

"Sure. Reena, Marsh didn't strike me as the kind of man who would pay for sex. More the kind who'd intimidate for it. I only met him a few days before he died, but I—"

"I know. The cops tried to get me to say I'd heard Teri mention your name, but she didn't used to do that."

"Do what?"

"Mention the name of her clients. To me, anyway. It was like a professional thing with her. Like confidentiality with a lawyer."

I considered it. "Then how did you know who Marsh was when the cops first contacted you?"

"I didn't. Till the drugs came into it. Then I knew who they meant."

"How?"

"Teri was into trading, you know? Like, what's the word for it, one thing for another?"

"Barter?"

"Yeah, barter. Right. She didn't have any kind of health plan, obviously, and she wasn't about to go to this butcher Niño knew, so there was this doctor she used to . . . do things for in exchange for his treating her. Well, I knew she was seeing a guy she got drugs from, cocaine, and when the cops asked me about Marsh, I just matched him up."

"She ever talk about him? The drug supplier, I mean?"

"No. She really didn't do that. At least not with me."

I thought about the next question I wanted to ask, because I was afraid that it might end her cooperation. "Reena, you said before that Teri approached you because you looked kind. She must have confided in somebody about some things."

"Maybe her sister. Teri never told me her name, always just 'my sister.' The family lives in Epton, near Lawrence." Reena stopped, then said, "I don't think you understand how it was between Teri and me."

"I guess I thought you were lovers."

Reena's eyes clouded over, but she spoke past them. "I loved her, but she came to me for the same reason clients came to her. To get something they were missing in the rest of their lives. I wish to God I knew what it was."

"Does Teri's sister still live at home?"

"You mean in Epton?"

"Yes."

"No, I don't think so. She's younger than Teri . . . than Teri was. But she'll be there today, anyway. The funeral was scheduled for this morning." Reena glanced up to a clock, and the tears began to come. "It started . . . ten minutes ago . . . I couldn't go . . . they've been through so much already. It didn't seem fair . . . to add me to it."

"It takes a pretty strong person to do something like that."

"Oh yeah," she said, rallying a little. "That's what

I've always been. Strong, tough even. Well, I'll tell you, you know some people are tougher than they look?"

"Yes."

"Well, I'm the opposite. I look tougher than I am."

I left her wiping a cuff across her eyes.

SIXTEEN

$\spadesuit$

I was unsteady getting up from the flowers and caught my balance by using her stone.

Too much to drink last night?

"No. Too much Terdell."

As the morning sun skipped over the waves in the harbor below us, I brought her up to date on what had happened.

So what do you think?

"I think I have a sackful of people who knew either Marsh or Teri but so far no connection between them."

How do you mean?

"Well, whoever hit me on Monday knew I'd be a good candidate for the frame. That means that somebody trying to kill Angel would have to know about me and Marsh."

What if just Marsh was the target?

"Then Teri's side of this is a blind alley. And I'm left with looking for motives for killing Marsh. I think his lawyer Felicia bought drugs from him, his partner Stansfield cashed a quarter-million in key-man insurance, and his wife Hanna believed she'd get both life-policy proceeds and the house."

The nurse's father hated Marsh, right?

"Yes, but Kelley seemed pretty quick to yield to his daughter's will when I was with him. Also, she alibis him for Monday night."

The drug pushers are rough enough.

"The problem there is that J.J. would be better off if Marsh had stayed alive. And none of the cops seem interested in anything but themselves or nailing me."

What about this Niño guy?

"Harder to figure. No indication that he even knew Marsh. Niño may have a nose for the stuff himself, or just be looking for indirect compensation for losing Teri. Or . . ."

Or?

"I don't know. Maybe he really cared for her. Her lover certainly did. And would have had the physical strength to send Marsh out the window."

And shoot the woman she loved in the bargain?

"You're right. Doesn't figure that way."

If Marsh didn't meet Teri through her manager, then maybe you should find out how they did get together.

"I've been trying to."

What are you going to do next?

"First, try to talk with Teri's sister."

Couldn't that wait?

"I don't even know her name or where she lives. If I'm going to see her, today at the family's house is the best bet."

You said first?

"What?"

You said first you were going to talk with the sister. Then what?

"Oh. Then I get to have lunch with Niño and his ladies."

I'd always heard that widowers were corruptible.

"Please."

The drive to Epton took about an hour. I'd looked up the family name in the telephone book, and it was the only one in town. A stop at a gas station pointed me toward the street, and the center of gravity of the dozen or so cars parked along the road appeared to be the address.

I slowed down. The shallow lawn rose steeply to the stoop. The inner door to the house was open but the outer, screened door was closed, the upper part filled by the broad back of a man in a dark suit. He seemed to be talking to someone, then swiveled sideways to let a young woman in a knee-length black dress edge past him and outside. She clicked down the path in modest heels, face downcast and palms locked onto elbows.

An old woman fussedly came halfway out the doorway and yelled something at her in Greek. This one wore black too, only more so: shoes, stockings, long skirt, sweater, even kerchief on her head. The younger woman ignored her, the older one giving a curiously European "good riddance" wave before going back into the house.

I pulled by the younger one. Her features matched the ones I'd seen in Holt's mug shot of Teri, but plainer and somehow less vital, the way a Xerox of a Xerox used to look.

She reached the sidewalk and turned to walk in the direction I was driving. I accelerated to the first empty stretch of curb and parked. I got out of the car and came around to the passenger side while she was still twenty feet away. Drawing closer, she treated me warily, as though she had just noticed me standing there. I could see her left hand: no engagement or wedding ring.

"Ms. Papangelis?"

"Yes?"

I showed her my ID quickly as I said, "My name's Cuddy. I'm investigating the death of your sister."

She sighed and closed her eyes. "Again?"

"I'm afraid so."

She opened her eyes and gestured vaguely behind her. "Today?"

"The sooner we get all the information we can, the better our chances of—"

"Okay, okay." She looked up the street. "Would it be all right if we just walked around for a while? I'm kind of tired of the house and all."

"Sure."

We continued on the route she'd started, past the old homes with narrow driveways and detached rear garages that could have been in any blue-collar neighborhood within fifty miles.

"Ask your questions."

"We still don't know for sure whether the killer was after Marsh or your sister. Can I call her Teri?"

"Theresa. You can call me Sandy or Sandra, I don't care. But Teri was her . . . the name she used with her customers. I always called her Theresa."

"It might help us focus on who was the target if you can tell me something about her."

"Like what? I mean, I already answered all the questions you guys had the last time."

"Tell me what you haven't said already. What you think I ought to know."

"God. What you ought to know." She took a breath.

"There were just the two of us, we had a brother, but he died while he was being born. Theresa was five years older than me, and always in trouble. I mean like school trouble, grades and attendance and that kind of thing. I was always the perfect student, skipped two grades, my father scraped and saved to send me through parochial school, you know? He would have done the same for Theresa, but she didn't care, and probably didn't have the aptitude to do the work. So she went one way and I went another."

"Which way did you go?"

"Teachers' college. Framingham State. Got out last year, now I'm teaching in Salem. Salem, New Hampshire, not Massachusetts."

"Did you stay in touch with your sister much?"

"Depends on how you mean. She and Mom don't . . . didn't get along too well. When she found out about what Theresa was doing . . ."

"When was that? That your mother found out."

"Not really till all this. I mean, my father suspected, for a long time, I think. But my mom . . . do you know much about Greek families?"

I thought back to what Eleni had told me about the men she hated in Greece. "Not much."

"Well, it's no disgrace for a man to go see a . . . they'd use the word 'whore.' The men joke about it in the living room, while the women make believe they can't hear them from the kitchen. But it's a real disgrace for your daughter to turn into one. That's one of the reasons I had to get out of the house just now. I couldn't stand the hypocritical men standing around trying to console my parents about what Theresa had become while they were probably kicking themselves for never trying to . . . never trying to see her, too."

"Tell me about Theresa personally."

"Personally?"

"Yes. What was she like?"

"Pretty. No, more flashy, like the kind of girl the guys would always be watching. She knew it, too. And she had this great smile and way of talking to you, that made you feel better even though it wasn't so much what she said as what she let you say." Sandra smiled, but it didn't make her look happy or pretty. "Maybe that's why she was good at what she did."

"You ever meet Roy Marsh?"

"No. To be honest, I'd really only see Theresa when she'd come up to the house for family stuff. Dinner once in a while, holidays. She never brought anybody with her. Or invited us down for anything. I don't think my parents ever even saw her apartment." She broke off, her expression hardening. "You guys decided when I can finally get in there and get her stuff?"

I remembered lunch with Niño and his possibly taking me there. "Not up to me. The one to call is Lieutenant Holt. Try him tomorrow and he'll probably okay it."

"So long as I can get in by the weekend. I want this all . . . all cleaned up by then."

"I can understand that. Did Theresa ever talk with you about her clients?"

"No. I know she had a guy managing for her. She took up with him after she had the trouble in Salem. And there were a couple of other girls working with her for him. But I don't remember their names." She half laughed. "Probably only heard their street names anyway."

"You said she got into trouble where you work?"

"Where I . . . oh, no. Not up there. Salem, Massachusetts. She got arrested, for soliciting I guess they call it. But that was a long time ago. I was just, what, maybe thirteen."

"Anything happen from it?"

155

"I don't think so, but I was kind of young to really understand, and she didn't exactly talk about it at the dinner table, you know?"

"She ever talk about leaving, about finding another line of work?"

The half-laugh again. "Not exactly. She always wanted to be a movie star. Even when she did go to school, she never really studied, just came home and read the fan magazines. She thought she looked like a young Natalie Wood. That was how she said it too, 'a young Natalie Wood.' She kept thinking that somehow she'd be able to get into movies through somebody she'd meet. How she thought that was going to happen for her when she lived here instead of out in California someplace . . ."

We'd made a circuit of the block and were drawing even with her parents' driveway.

She said, "Any more questions for me?"

"Not for now. I'm really sorry about Theresa."

Sandra kicked a stone off the sidewalk and onto her father's lawn. "Save your sympathy for Teri. She's the one who died Monday. Theresa I lost a long time ago."

She turned away from me and walked resignedly back up the path to the house.

"John! Christ, I haven't seen you in, what, five years."

"More like seven, Ed."

I grew up in South Boston with Ed. He'd wanted to attend college and law school, but his steady girlfriend's pregnancy intervened. Starting out as a night janitor in the South Boston courthouse, he slowly moved up the chain to an assistant clerk's job. He's active in court administration across the Commonwealth and knows everybody.

"What brings you back to God's Little Acre? Oh, shit," he said, striking himself on the forehead with the palm of his hand. "I forgot about Beth. I'm sorry."

"No need to be sorry. I'm here officially. Sort of."

Ed leaned over the counter and looked in every direction before saying, "What's the trouble?"

"You know the killing over at the Barry?"

"Just what I read in the *Herald*. A hooker and her john, right?"

"Right. My gun was found at the scene, and I need some information I can't look up for myself."

"Christ, John. A double murder, that's pretty heavy stuff. How deep are you in this?"

"I didn't do it. Somebody mugged me and took my gun to frame me."

"The paper just said something about 'unidentified' weapon."

"Yeah, but it's not the weapon I'm interested in. It's the hooker."

"I don't get it."

"I'm told she was in some legal trouble a while back."

"And that surprises you?"

"No, but I can't go through the cops for the story."

"I don't know, John. All that shit is tied up by the privacy statute. The records, I mean. She processed through here?"

"No. Salem District Court."

"Salem! Christ, John, the chief judge of the whole fucken system works outta Salem."

"Ed, you've shaken every hand ever stamped a paper in this state. All I need is some noncontroversial information about her."

"Like what?"

"One of the suspects is a lawyer from Marblehead

157

who used to do a lot of criminal work. I want to see if she was involved in the case."

"Why—never mind. I don't wanna know." Ed bothered his teeth with his tongue for a while. "I don't know, John. How long ago was all this?"

"Eight years, give or take."

"Oh, John, all the stuff from that far back'd be on the micro." He made a rude noise. "Okay, I'll give it a try. But I'm gonna have to bury this with some other kinda requests, and God save the sailor if anybody ever notices who was asking about her."

"I really appreciate it, Ed."

"Name?"

"Street name was Teri Angel. Real name, and probably the one Salem would have, is Papangelis, Theresa."

"Spell it for me."

I spelled it. "Age back then about nineteen. The lawyer's name is Felicia Arnold."

"Gimme a couple days. I'll call you."

"Thanks, Ed."

"Christ," he said walking away. "Guys lose their pensions like this."

SEVENTEEN

La Flor was tucked between a mom-and-pop *grocería* and a dry cleaner's on the lower end of Sommer Street. I parked two doors down from the cleaner's and watched the front door of the restaurant for a while. Two construction workers in bandanas, boots, and nonmatching hard hats came out, chewing thoughtfully on toothpicks. Not seeing anybody else by 1:30, I got out of the Fiat and walked into the place.

There were twenty small tables crammed into the bowling alley space that reminded me more of New York than Boston. The tables were draped in clean white cloths, a fresh-cut carnation in a clear glass vase centered on each. An elderly couple were finishing lunch near the window. She wore a plain print dress, he a fifties sharkskin suit. They were holding hands and toasting each other with small port glasses.

Niño waved to me from the back of the room. He sat on one of three stools at a tiny bar, behind which a fat man was drying glasses with a towel. Immediately in front of Niño was a table for four with two women eating across from each other. One had a badly bleached ponytail draped across her near shoulder, the other long raven black hair. They both glanced up at me, the blonde following me with her eyes as I walked toward them, the other just returning to her plate.

Niño slid off the barstool. The women both looked about thirty. Given their working hours, they could have been anywhere from seventeen to forty. The blonde was tall, even sitting down, and heavily made up. The other slumped in her chair and wore no cosmetics at all. As I reached the table, the blonde smiled at me in a practiced way, the other paid no attention.

Niño said, "John Cuddy, I have the pleasure of giving you Maylene and Salomé."

The blonde said, "I'm Maylene, honey." She had a south of Kansas twang in her voice. "I show it, I shake it, and I share it."

Salomé, out of the corner of her mouth, said, "Jesus."

Niño said, "You and me sit here and here, John. You know, boy, girl, boy, girl?"

I sat down, Maylene to my left, Salomé to my right. "Has Niño told you why I wanted to talk with you?"

Maylene said, "Yeah. It's about the Angel." She laid her hand over mine and gripped tight. "God, I was terrified when I heard."

Salomé seemed awfully bored. Her attitude reminded me of the bare tolerance an experienced cop shows when paired with a rookie. I put Salomé nearer forty, Maylene nearer seventeen.

Niño said, "Hey, John, you making some impression here. I think Maylene want to swallow you pride."

Maylene took her hand off mine and gently slapped Niño on the shoulder in that limp-wristed way some women use to show tenderness. Niño took it playfully. Salomé broke off another piece of bread from the shallow basket in front of her and sopped some gravy from her dish.

"Niño, I'd really like to talk with the women alone, okay?"

He shook his head, but he stood up. "You really think they tell you something they don't tell me after you leave?"

"Who can say?"

Niño picked up his drink and said, "I order you the *arroz con pollo* and some white wine. The chicken and rice the spec-i-al-ity of the house." He looked from Salomé to Maylene and back again. "You ladies tell this man anything he want to know."

Maylene said, "Yes, Niño." Salomé finished her hunk of bread while Maylene struggled to lift her handbag onto the table. Made from natural cowhide, it had outlandish fringes, the kind of present Dale Evans might have bought Buttermilk for Mother's Day.

Waiting till Niño resumed his seat at the bar, I decided to start with Maylene. I figured Salomé would know more that would help me, but I doubted she'd talk until she'd become fed up with Maylene.

"How close were you to Teri Angel?"

Maylene frowned, as though that wasn't the question for which she'd prepared an answer. "I wouldn't say close. The Angel didn't want anybody to be close, I don't think."

"Why was that?"

Maylene took a pack of cigarettes from her bag. Her hands were big and rough, almost manly. "I don't know. She really wouldn't let any of the girls get to know her. Not like Salomé and me."

Salomé avoided laughing by taking a swig of wine.

"You ever meet anybody with her?"

"You mean like a date or something?"

"Yeah."

"No. Really, we don't . . . didn't see her that much. Just here and other places for lunch once in a while."

"Why is that?"

"Well, Niño sets us up through these hotel people he knows, so we're mainly on with convention types in the afternoons and maybe some traveling executives like at night. We just do one-ons."

"One-ons?"

Salomé groaned and said, "She means one-on-ones. No parties or group gigs."

"Oh."

Maylene said, "That's why we wouldn't see her except at lunch here sometimes. We just weren't together when we were working. We weren't . . . aren't even supposed to say hi to each other if we see a girl in the hotels or anything."

"Because of their security people?"

"Right."

The fat man came toward us, carrying my chicken dish and a half-carafe of wine. Given the timing, I was pretty sure La Flor didn't exactly cook to order. I tried it. Not bad.

"Did you know any of her free-lance clients?"

Salomé laughed. "You don't know a hell of a lot about the life, do you?"

"No."

"Well, I got a client expecting my Dance of the Seven Veils in about an hour, and I gotta get painted and changed by then, so let me save you some time, okay?"

"Okay." I took more chicken.

"You're in the life for a while, you got two choices. Get out, or get your own."

"Your own prostitutes?"

"No. Oh, that too, yeah. If you can stand dealing with pompom girls."

Maylene said, "Sal! You promised never to tell any—"

"So let's say you don't want to be Niño the Second. You gotta get your own book of clients. Free-lance, okay?"

"Got it," I said around my chewing.

"Now, you get the right book of clients, you can be pretty well set. Lots of these guys are just looking for somebody reliable, you know?" Salomé cranked up her tempo, an enthusiastic broker describing a property with potential. "Somebody who'll do the things for them that the wives won't without gagging and bitching about it. They find a girl they like, they're loyal like fucking football fans about it. They stick with the same girl for years. God, I know a girl has the same three lawyers for fifteen years. Fifteen fucking *years*. They all know each other, but nobody knows they're all doing her except her. She covers all her overhead on those three guys alone, and that's just twice a month each."

"So?"

Salomé slowed down. "So, a girl gets a good free-lance, she ain't about to spread that information around to her competitors, follow?"

"I thought you said the free-lance clients were loyal?"

"Yeah, but they ain't perfect. If they were, they wouldn't be clients to start with."

"So you never saw her book?"

"What book?"

"Her book of free-lancers."

"Jesus. I didn't mean she had a *book*. That'd be stupid."

"Why?"

"Because they call her, not the other way around. Besides, if you did have a book, you couldn't carry it with you, because the cops'd grab it, and you couldn't leave it at your place, because your pimp would read it."

I looked over at Niño. Maylene said quickly, "Oh, Niño wouldn't do something like that."

Sal said, "Maylene, grow up or shut up."

I said, "Niño doesn't mind you all branching out?"

"No." This time Salomé glanced over at him and couldn't quite hide a crinkle of genuine affection. "No, Niño's good that way. Steers us the business, takes his cut but lets us keep the lion's share. And, he doesn't muscle in with the free-lancers. He understands how it is."

"Any of Teri's clients go in for rough stuff?"

"No way. First of all, Teri had the looks, way too good to need the rough boys. Plus, you don't keep that kind of action as a free-lance. You need your man around to keep them in line sometimes."

"So Teri didn't talk with you about her free-lancers."

Maylene seemed eager to contribute. "Well, she did, sort of."

"How do you mean?"

"Well, she talked about her sources."

"Her sources?"

"Yeah, where she got the free-lances from. Like sometimes one client refers another to her. And then she had this lawyer who did a lot of divorce stuff, the lawyer would send the husbands to Teri for, well, kind of like that Masters and Jones stuff?"

Salomé said, "Masters and Johnson."

Maylene said, "Yeah, them."

"Teri ever mention the lawyer's name?"

"No, just that it was a girl. A woman lawyer, I mean. Teri never mentioned names or anything, but she'd talk about some of them like that."

"Like what?"

"Like give them made-up names, you know?"

"Like street names?"

"No, no. More like . . ."

Salomé said, "Labels. Like 'the Senator,' 'the Wizard'—"

"He was like a computer genius, the Wizard—"

"—'the Producer,' and like that."

I thought about sister Sandra mentioning Teri's interest in the movies. "What did she mean by 'the Producer'?"

Salomé said, "Not the real thing. Not Hollywood, I mean. She just had some guy liked to look at himself getting done. He took movies of it."

"Movies of him and Teri together?"

"That's what she said."

"Videocamera?"

Salomé took a cigarette from Maylene's pack and lit up. "How else you gonna make them?"

"Did Teri ever mention anything else about this Producer?"

Salomé blew a cone of smoke sideways from her mouth and away from me. "No."

Maylene said, "But Sal—"

"She didn't say anything else, Maylene."

"She did, though." Maylene turned to me and elaborately away from Salomé's glare. "The Producer was her candy man."

165

"Drugs."

"Right. As much as she wanted, although she never used a lot."

"She ever describe him?"

"Like what he looked like and all?"

"Yeah."

"No—yeah, wait, she did! She said he had these tattoos. Like of a tank or something."

No question we were talking about Marsh now. "Did she see this guy on a regular basis?"

"Yeah, sure."

"Same time and place each week?"

"Oh, I don't know about that. She did say . . . Sal, when did we have lunch with her that last time?"

"I don't remember."

"Sure you do. It was . . . no, no, it wasn't here. It was down at the Market."

"Quincy Market?"

"Yeah, yeah. Right down by the water. And she said . . . no, no, it wasn't lunch, it was brunch. Remember, Sal, we couldn't get served our drinks 'cause it wasn't twelve noon yet?"

"I don't remember."

"Sure you do. We wanted Bloody Marys, and the waiter said we had to wait, and Teri joked about taking care of him if he'd take care of us, but you could see he was a fag so he didn't think she was funny."

"What did she tell you?"

"About the Producer?"

"Yes."

"Just that she was going to do a screen test."

"Screen test?"

"Yeah, you know, like an audition, only for the movies. She thought the way she could get into the movies was to be in one of those porno things, and the

Producer told her he knew somebody who did them. He was the candy man, so maybe he did, I don't know."

"And he was going to introduce her to this real movie guy?"

"Yeah. Well, no. No, I think what she said was that the real movie guy would want a sample of what she could do." Maylene put her hand to her mouth and giggled. "I don't mean that way, in person. I mean on film. How she'd look doing it."

"With one of the guys she free-lanced?"

"Yeah. Or one of the girls."

"One of you?"

"No, no. I mean one of her girl clients. Some of the lezzies, they really go for somebody as beautiful as the Angel. And even the straight ones, they like to try some new things, if you get me."

"So the Producer was going to arrange some kind of screen test for Teri."

"Right."

"When?"

Maylene frowned again, straining to remember. "I don't think she said, but I think it was supposed to be real soon."

"Soon?"

"After we were talking. She said she'd seen the Producer like the night before."

"And when was that?"

"At the brunch, like I said."

"Yes, but when was the brunch?"

"When?" She looked at Salomé, then back to me. "On Sunday. When else do you have brunch?"

"You mean this past Sunday?"

"Yeah, yeah."

The day before she was killed.

* * *

167

SWAN DIVE

After I was finished with Maylene and Salomé, the fat man bowed to me graciously and said he hoped I'd enjoyed my meal. On my way to the door, Niño told me he'd meet me outside Teri Angel's apartment house at 8:00. He gave me the address, a building down by the waterfront.

I climbed into the Fiat, drove across the MassPike interchange and into Back Bay. Heading downtown, I wended my way through the construction on Boylston Street and then quartered over past the New England School of Law and Tufts Medical and Dental complexes. The Barry Hotel stood a bit farther toward the Fort Point Channel and near South Station, railroads being the principal mode of transportation back when the Barry was Queen of the Hub.

"Hope there're no hard feelings about yesterday?"

The little guy in the bellboy outfit had a sincere look in his remaining eye, the patch on the other one tied on jauntily with black, woven cords. The man with the pop-bottle glasses was dozing behind the registration desk across the lobby.

"No hard feelings," I said, resting my elbow on the top of the wooden captain's stand. "Thanks for not identifying me as the bad guy."

"Hah," he said, unnecessarily shuffling some blank forms on the writing area in front of him. "You ain't exactly the sort we cater to nowadays."

He moved his head around, sweeping quickly over the tattered carpet, worn upholstery, and sallow wallpaper. He made a clucking sound with his tongue against his teeth. "You also ain't old enough to remember her in her glory, but this dowdy bitch was a hell of a hotel once."

I stuck out my hand. "John Cuddy."

168

"Name on my discharge papers is Norbert, Olin C. But everybody calls me Patch. Bet ya can't guess why."

I laughed politely and let him go on.

"Lost the eye right near the end of things, when the Japs were trying to kill us and themselves with the kamikazes. Hit the ship, but we managed to save her. Didn't have no medical attention for six hours, but the doc said six minutes wouldn't have made any difference. Fire flash seared the lens part right off. But I got no complaints, the VA takes care of me, and the disability pension plus this place pay me as much as I'll ever need."

"How'd you come to be here?"

"The hotel, you mean?"

"Yeah."

"We was here on liberty once. Boston, I mean. First time I ever seen a real city, being from Indiana bottomland originally. Also, right here's where I first got laid. Room seventeen-oh-four. Never will forget it. I thought about this place afterwards, while I was in the hospital. After I got out and all, I come here and they signed me on."

"Since the cops had you in for the show-up, I'm guessing you were on when Teri Angel was killed."

"Shit, son, I'm on pretty near every day."

"You remember her that night?"

"Nope. I knew which one she was, though. You ever see her?"

"Just a photo."

"Well, she was a beauty, that one. Not just the body, she had the face, too. Didn't look the same as the others somehow, like she didn't have the same hardness to her or something."

A black woman in a blond wig and purple hot pants

169

plowed past us, towing a fiftyish guy scratching his forehead to keep us from seeing his face clearly. They didn't bother stopping at the registration desk.

Patch gave me a look that said, "See what I mean."

"The police told me that somebody here recognized Roy Marsh as one of Teri's regular customers."

"That was me."

"You know her other regulars, too?"

"To be square with you, no, I can't say for sure. You see, I come on at three usually. I like my days off, go for walks, especially this time of year. So there could be a lot of guys—some women too, if you can believe it—who coulda been regulars and I'd never see 'em, or just see 'em coming or leaving and never with any particular girl."

"See any other regulars that night?"

"Of hers, you mean?"

"Yes."

"Nope."

"But you knew Marsh was one of hers for sure."

"Yeah. Well, I didn't know his name till the cops told me. It ain't exactly the sort of thing we wanta keep track of, get me?"

"You saw her with him?"

"Once. And I'd see him sometimes on days I knew she was entertaining."

"You the one who saw him with the suitcase?"

"Right. Both times."

"Both times?"

"Yeah. I saw him with it maybe six, eight months ago, then again on Monday night."

"Eight months ago?"

"Give or take."

That was way before any of the divorce stuff.

"Any idea what was in the suitcase?"

Patch smiled knowingly. "Nope. And around here, you don't ask."

"What are my chances of seeing the room?"

Patch crossed his arms, doing a slow-motion dance with his feet. "No chance at all. The cops are pretty good about not bothering us here. So when something happens, we cooperate like goddamn boy scouts. They say nobody goes in the room, nobody gets in."

"What does a room rent for here?"

"Ten bucks."

"An hour."

"Uh-huh."

"There another room like the one she died in?"

"Sure. Any of the oh-twos."

"The what?"

"The oh-twos. Like nine-oh-two, ten-oh-two, get it? She was killed in twelve-oh-two, and all of them are like identical above and below."

"How about I reserve eleven-oh-two upfront for a coupla hours, but use it only for about twenty minutes?"

"Alone?"

"No. You as my tour guide."

He smiled and said, "Elevator on the right. Watch your step, please."

"Anything different?"

Patch looked around 1102. Swaybacked double bed, bureau that looked like the backstop at an archery range, a couple of faded prints on the wall, one in a frame with cracked glass. "Can't swear about the prints, but the furniture is all like twelve-oh-two's."

"In the same relative position in the room?"

"Yup."

I walked to the window. The sill was old-fashioned,

beginning just above my knee, the glass rising nearly six feet high. Patch said, "That's where he went out. Up a floor, of course."

The view was the South Station coupling yards, two locomotives desultorily warming up or cooling down. Must have been a damned impressive sight in the forties, though I doubted Marsh appreciated the historical perspective.

In addition to the entrance, there were two big doors off the room, one next to the bed, the other past the footboard. Each looked to be of solid wood with glass knobs.

I looked into the one at the footboard first. Just a hopper and a sink within the loosely tiled walls. "Only a half bath?"

"The oh-twos used to be suites. Then they broke 'em up. Didn't put showers and all in most of them."

I moved to the other door. Patch whisked it open for me. "The spacious walk-in closet."

Four feet by five. A horizontal bar at eye level, some wire hangers on it. An old baggage holder with two of three straps broken. I said, "This where they found Marsh's wallet?"

"So they tell me. After he hit the ground, some guy off the street comes running in, saying there was somebody splattered all over the goddamn pavement. I run out after him. There's a body all right. Kind of. Haven't seen such a mess since the war. It looks to me like her regular 'cause of the short hair, but Karl—he's the guy with the thick cheaters—he goes all to pieces, so he's no good, and I gotta call the cops, then go out and make sure nobody fools around with what's left of this guy Marsh until they get here."

"So you weren't in a position to see who was leaving the hotel?"

"Son, like I told the cops, with the commotion from

the sirens and all, you gotta understand, a lot of people in beds in this place ain't planning to sleep over. The joint cleared out like one of them old-time cartoons of the rats leaving the ship, you know? Like in speeded-up motion?"

"Did you see the actual scene in twelve-oh-two?"

Patch sighed. "Yeah. After the cops got here and secured things in the street, I pointed up to the window. You could see it was broke 'cause of the way the lights from the yards across there didn't shine off it. I brought one of them, the Guinness guy was with you yesterday morning, I brought him up to twelve-oh-two and let him in. He told me to stay outside, and I did, but I could see the girl, down by the bed there."

Patch swung his index finger left to right from the bed up to the wall near the closet door. "So much blood and the way she was lying, you could tell she was dead."

I walked around the room one more time. It wasn't telling me anything. I thanked Patch and left.

EIGHTEEN

◆

I got back to the condominium about 4:00 P.M. My office answering service gave me the same two messages that my home tape machine had. Hanna Marsh and J.J. Braxley. I called Hanna first at the Swampscott number.

"Hello?"

"Hanna, this is John Cuddy, returning your call."

"Oh, thank you. Two men come here to see me."

"Who?"

"Two black men. They say that Roy was in business with them."

Here we go. "When was this?"

"This morning. Before lunch."

"What did they want?"

"They want something they said Roy had. They didn't say the drugs, but I knew that was what they meant. I told them I knew nothing, I was not with Roy

174

then or before even. The man with kind of funny hair just smiled. The other, he didn't say nothing but he smelled so bad."

"Did they threaten you?"

"No. Well, no, they didn't make to hit me or nothing. I looked through the window when they ring the bell, so I send Vickie upstairs where they can't see her."

Out of sight wasn't exactly out of mind. "What did they do?"

"Nothing I could tell the police or anybody. Just that they wanted the—the smiling one called it 'the material'—the material back or else they would have to 'pursue other alternations' or something like that."

"Hanna, listen. If they're willing to visit you in broad daylight, they're not planning on doing anything just yet. They also probably expected you to call me, which means they'll want to give me time to find the drugs for them."

"So you think Vickie and I are safe?"

"For a while, anyway. Still, better keep Vickie around you a little closer than usual, okay?"

"Okay. John?"

"Yes?"

"I thank you for helping us, but please don't get hurt again."

"Don't worry. I'll be careful."

I rang off and dialed the number J.J. had left. A crusty voice said, "Yeah?"

"Can I talk with J.J. Braxley?"

"Who want him?"

"The guy he called."

"J.J., he call lotsa folk."

It didn't sound like Terdell, so I said, "Look, pal, tell you what. You tell J.J. that the guy he wanted to talk to spoke to you and you fucked it up. Or I can mention it to J.J. the next time I see him."

"You lookin' to end up—"

"Because I'm pretty sure he'll know it was you, since he really needs to talk to me and he left me this number to call, which means he probably knows that you're always around to answer it."

Some hesitation, then barely civilly, "He got the number you at?"

"He's got two of them. Let him guess which one'll be good for fifteen more minutes."

"Hey, I don't—"

I hung up on him. No more than five minutes later, the telephone rang.

"This is John Cuddy."

"Mon, you think you a pretty slick dude."

"Let's just say I'm not too impressed by the quality of your staff."

"My staff, huh? My staff Terdell, he like to know exactly what happen last night."

"Hard to say. I was delirious."

"Terdell, he not too smart to start with. Last night didn't improve things none."

"They can do wonders nowadays with learning disabilities."

"Oh, mon. Two quality players like you and me, we shouldn't be all the time fighting. We got lots of things to talk about, be beneficent to both of us."

"I guess I wouldn't have called last night so beneficent."

"My mistake. Don't like to admit to such things generally, but I approach you all wrong. Didn't realize your depth."

"Why don't we cut the crap, all right? I've got other calls to make."

"I expect you do at that. I want another meet, try a different approach this time."

"What about?"

"I tell you when I see you."

"You're wasting my time, J.J."

"You pick the time and the place. And I guarantee it won't be no waste."

"Okay. Half an hour. Bar on Boylston Street called J.C. Hillary's."

"I be there."

"Better leave Terdell in the car. Unless you've had him hermetically sealed."

"You not exactly on Terdell's kiss list, mon. I'd walk wide around him, I was you."

"Half an hour."

I hung up and debated with myself for all of ten seconds before punching Murphy's office number.

"Lieutenant Murphy."

"Lieutenant, John Cuddy."

"Cuddy, I told you already. I can't talk with you."

"Then talk with your buddy Sergeant Dawkins. Tell him I'm meeting Braxley at Braxley's request at J.C. Hillary's in thirty minutes."

"The one on Boylston?"

"Right."

"You got something going with Dawkins, why don't you call him yourself?"

"Because he didn't dress like he hung around his office much. Besides, I think I'm going to want a council of war tomorrow with Holt, and I know where his office is."

"I'm not even gonna ask why the hell you don't call Holt then."

"Be back to you tonight."

"I'll be in Saint Croix by then."

Murphy hung up. I was glad to see him regaining his sense of humor.

J.J. came through the heavy front doors by himself. I was seated at the bar. He casually looked around, the place nearly empty at 4:30, as the convention facility across the street was under construction. He walked over to me and said, "How about we take us a table?"

I led him to a back corner. We sat and the waitress took his order for Chivas on the rocks while I sipped my screwdriver.

When she moved away, he said, "Smart. You picking a place this public and this confidential, all at the same time."

I raised my drink, turning the glass slowly in my hand. "I picked this place because they use fresh-squeezed orange juice in their cocktails."

Braxley gave me a barracuda grin. "You a little more than I bargain for, Cuddy."

"How do you mean?"

"I figure, mon so dumb he get whomped on the head and lose his piece, that mon be a little easier to push."

"I take it you finally buy my version of what happened?"

The waitress brought his drink. He worked his smile on her, but got nothing in return. He hooded his eyes, tossed off half the drink, then settled back.

"I don't buy nothing. I already bought. Bought and paid for the stuff Marsh had on him."

"I think we already had this conversation."

"Oh no, mon. Not this conversation. Last night just an exhibition compared to what come."

"You make me too nervous, I might spill my drink on you."

178

"No, my friend. What come ain't gonna come on you. I watch just now, coming over to the table here. You move pretty good for what Terdell whale upon you last night. You gotta hurt, nobody take that and not hurt, but you cover it. That mean you can take a lot more, and probably be real careful not to get suckered like we do last night. No, I was not thinking on you."

"Your visit to Hanna Marsh?"

Braxley looked pleased. "Thought she be calling about that."

"She doesn't know where the drugs are. She had nothing to do with Marsh for a while before he died."

"I believe her."

"So?"

"So, I visiting not to see the woman so much as the house. Saw it once before, but that was in the night, time we paid Marsh himself a little visit."

"The one that put him in the hospital?"

"Marsh, he made of milk, mon. Can't take the lickin' like you."

"Didn't you get a good look at it the time you and Terdell tossed it?"

"Just Terdell that time."

"Maybe if you got to the point?"

Braxley lapped a little more scotch. "Thought you be smart enough to see the point."

"I've always been disappointing that way."

"Maybe I better sharpen the matter up for you then." He put down the glass with a flourish. "I get the stuff from my supplier, I pay him. I give the stuff to Marsh, he don't pay me. The word is out on the street. 'J.J. get the sting,' 'J.J. give the credit and get burned,' and like that. But the stuff, it ain't on the street. That don't ring true. Some people get ideas, think maybe

I'm gone soft about things. Business things. Somebody work up the balls to try me, see if I push a little on the territory. Means I gotta push back. Inefficient. Waste my resources on fights I don't want and can't make pay."

Braxley affected a woeful look, playing to the second balcony. "Or maybe my supplier talk to one of these dudes, get the word that I'm loose with his shit, he think, 'Fuck, J.J. slipping the knot, getting ready to bolt on me, gotta groom this new J.J., take his place.' Then I push the new man, supplier say, 'Fuck is this shit? What the hell J.J. doing?' Then the supplier, he ask himself, 'How come the last load ain't hit the street yet?' I don't need those kinds of troubles, mon."

"Sounds like you got them. Through your own fault with Marsh."

The woeful look dissolved. "Sound that way to you? Well, let's us see how this sound. I give Marsh the credit, he don't pay up. He do that to a bank, what the bank do?"

I didn't respond. Braxley reached for his drink and finished it decisively.

"Tell you what the bank do. The bank treat that like a family obligation, mon. The bank go take his house and toss his family on the street. Well, you talking to a bank now, the First National Bank of Braxley. Terdell and me visit the missus this morning, polite as can be. We wearing hats, they woulda been in our hands. We give her notice this morning, but I spell it out for you. I get back my shit, or we take the house to cover it."

"You ever hear of duress?"

Braxley started to laugh, then cut it off. "'Duress,' huh? That woman own that house now, she can do whatever she want with it. Like she can put it on the market for maybe twenty thousand less than it worth,

180

and sell it like in a few weeks, and she get plenty on it, mon, plenty enough to cover her husband's debt. And she gonna wanna do it, too. Know why?"

I still didn't say anything.

"Sure you know why. You just don't wanna hear the words in the air. You a sensitive son of a bitch. Well, maybe you better brace yourself, 'cause here they come, ready or not. She gonna wanna do that for me because I like be holding her little child in excrow. The daughter she so careful not to let us see this morning. You know what excrow mean?"

"The expression is 'escrow,' Braxley, and I know what it means."

He sat back, even more pleased with himself. "You got the benefit of a fine stateside education, my friend. I just a poor immigrant, but I catch on fast. This here an open society, anything possible for a mon who willing. You believe it."

I believed it.

I waited in the bar for half an hour after J.J. left. Then I looped around the blocks the long way and drifted toward my building from the river side. No whiff of Terdell or sign of anyone else. I went inside and upstairs.

I called the Christideses' home number.

"Who is this?"

It sounded like one of Eleni's cousins, so I said, "My name is John Cuddy. Eleni wanted to see me yesterday."

I heard some muffled talk in Greek, then the voice came back to me with "Wait, wait, she come." I waited.

"John?"

"Yes, Eleni. Is everything all right?"

181

"Yes, fine, fine. You want Chris?"

"Please."

"He not here, John."

"I really need to speak with him. Do you know when he'll be back?"

"He gone to a meeting two hours already. Can he call you back?"

"Yes. I'll be home."

"I tell him."

I thanked her, pushed down the button, and called Murphy again.

"Murphy."

"Lieutenant, it's me, Cuddy."

"Hold on. Holt's right here."

"Lieutenant, wait—"

"Cuddy, this is Holt. Just what the hell you think you're pulling here?"

"Lieutenant, I'd like a meeting with you and Dawkins tomorrow."

"You fucken asshole. Where do you—"

"In the morning, if possible. Your office would be fine."

"How about I send a cruiser right now?"

"How about I call Senator Kennedy and tell him how you're violating my civil rights?"

"What rights?"

"You want to send a cruiser, fine. You want me to tell the papers and TV in a few days how you and yours were responsible for botching a double murder and getting a child hurt on top of it, go ahead."

"What child? The fuck are you talking about?"

"I'll explain it tomorrow. How about ten A.M.?"

The gnashing of teeth. "You be here. If we are, too, we'll hear what you have to say."

I put the receiver down and turned on the news. I sat through sports, weather, and Tom Brokaw. Then I went downstairs, backed the car out of the space, and drove to the waterfront.

Most of the residential housing on the harbor consists of condominium flats in redeemed warehouses. The warehouses themselves sit on wharves, huge stone and beam intrusions into the water and from another century. Before Boston's renaissance fifteen years ago, the wharves were abandoned, and only the intrepid would wade through the muddy moats the filled land around them had become. Ten thousand cash at a tax title auction would have snagged you a whole structure. Now, the same money would just about cover two years of property assessment on a single two-bedroom unit.

I slowly drove by the address Niño gave me. Teri's place was in one of the newly constructed towers, rising floors above even the elevated, six-laned Central Artery that still separates the docks from the commercial downtown. As I pulled over to come back around, I saw Niño get out of his parked Olds across the street and incline his head toward the building entrance. Five minutes later, I found a parking space and joined him.

He nodded approvingly. "Punc-tu-al-ity, man. At lunch and tonight, too. Important quality for professional men like you and me."

Niño was wearing brown suit pants with cuffs and Hush Puppies shoes, but it was the top half of his outfit that caught the eye. Blue dress shirt, pencil-width leather tie, and a starched white coat with "Dr. Rodriguez" stitched over the chest pocket. The earpieces of a stethoscope protruded from a side pocket.

"Career change?"

"You like the getup? Shit, man, this here a condo building. Half the units owned by fucken docs as tax shelters, you know it? I walk in like this, we blend in. Rent-a-cop figure, 'Big-time *médico,* too fucken cheap to have some agency show the place to a new tenant.' C'mon."

Niño pulled the door open for me, then moved in quickly and got ahead of me, marching along in that self-absorbed way you see in hospital corridors.

The guard said, "Evening, doctor."

Niño half saluted but never broke stride. I shrugged at the guard and whispered, "Famous surgeon."

The guard winked to show no offense taken.

Niño eased the door closed, pushing the police bar back into the slot on the floor.

I said, "That was easy."

"The cops, they don't post no round-the-clock shit for a dead hooker, man. Besides, she killed someplace else."

The room was a large L-shaped studio, sleeping alcove off to the right, bathroom and kitchenette to the left. Sweeping view of boat moorings and airport runways through the picture windows, a small telescope set up near the glass.

Niño walked toward the telescope, saying over his shoulder, "Do you thing, man. Just don't break nothing, okay?"

I started with the alcove. Cherrywood four-poster bed, frilly comforter, the collar of a flannel shirt just visible under one of the pillows. On cold nights, Teri probably slept in it. Beth used to do that all the time.

Matching nightstands flanked the headboard. On one of them sat a telephone and a tape machine identical to the one in my apartment. An "O" glowed in the message portal. I pushed the side button which releases the lid. Both outgoing and incoming tapes were still there. I moved the lever to "Answer Play," the device immediately rewinding the short distance with no noise. That meant the "O" wasn't kidding, buddy, there really were no messages. The machine automatically clicked to "Play" anyway, nothing but silence coming from the speaker. Stupid to think the cops hadn't already tried it.

"Hey, man, come look at this!"

I went into the living room portion, Niño bending over the telescope and adjusting some knob near his squinting eye. "This little mother is powerful. Planes, luggage carts, shit, I can see right into the terminals almost."

"Teri ever mention anything about the telescope?"

"Not to me. But she was weird that way. She give me the key to this place 'cause she trust me and somebody gotta have it, case she get the slam and all."

I thought about what Sandra had asked me. I'd gotten the impression that Teri had told her about the apartment and given her a key. Would Teri have given keys to both of them?

I went back into the sleeping area and toward the other nightstand. A Harlequin romance facedown, marking her place the hard way, binding nearly broken through. An ashtray, some kind of nail strengthener, china cup with coins and subway tokens in it.

"Niño, did Teri drive a car?"

"No. She knew how, but she didn't want to keep one in the city. She need one, she borrow mine or see the Hertz counter."

On the walls, a couple of Natalie Wood publicity stills, framed professionally. Below them, a bureau with an overload of cosmetic enhancers, most of which I couldn't identify without reading the fine print.

On either side of the cosmetics, two photos in stand-up Plexiglas functioned almost like bookends.

185

One was a staged pose of a young, dark couple dressed in the style of the early sixties. They stood behind two little girls sitting on a piano bench, party dresses, white socks, shiny black shoes with straps, and ankles crossed. The younger Sandra and Theresa, Sandra's smile shy, Theresa's bold. The other photo was a yearbook shot of Sandra, smile still shy, features unformed like the first sense I'd had of her outside the house in Epton. No yearbook photo of Theresa.

I opened each drawer in turn. The police would already have searched pretty thoroughly, so I just poked and peered a little. Mostly different kinds of strappie and tube tops with short shorts. Lingerie ranging from the erotic to the ridiculous. Some regular clothes too, though. Sweaters, polo shirts, Reebok sports shorts.

Behind me I heard, "Ooh, foxy lady, keep that light on! Hey man, you wanna catch some of this?"

I guessed he'd swung away from the airport. "No thanks."

"You missing academy award shit here, man. Ow, yes, yes."

I came into the living room area. Sectional furniture, nice rug, three-tiered coffee table of brass and glass. "Teri decorate herself?"

"She pick—oh, mama, I didn't know it could bend that way!—she like picked it out, but the landlord, he pay the freight."

"You know him?"

"No, just some dentist, pillar of his com-mun-i-ty somewhere in the suburbs. He rented the place to her himself. I think maybe she let him stick something in her mouth beside the little round mirror, you know it?"

I opened the sliding door to a wall-length closet. Lots of flash and sparkle, but also a tweed suit, a nun's habit, and a nurse's uniform. "Pretty varied wardrobe."

"Some of the johns, man, they like the ladies to dress up, fantasyland."

I thought about her coming home, hanging up an outfit after spending the day and most of the night with Niño's clients and her free-lances. I shook my head and walked into the bathroom. Typical modern job, clean and impersonal. "You have any idea where she kept her paperwork?"

"Paperwork?"

"Yeah. Bills, checkbooks, that kind of thing."

"The Angel, man, she was cash-and-carry. Fucken cops got all the papers she have, and probably stuffed in their wallets."

I came back into the living room area. "She must have had light bills, phone bills . . ."

Niño ignored me and began futzing with the lens again. I walked over to a sectional corner piece and sat down.

Niño said, "You just about done here?"

When I didn't answer him, he looked up. "Man?"

"I was just thinking."

"About what?"

"Teri, this apartment. Seems kind of an empty place to call home, and even this she paid for in kind."

Niño's face contorted for just a moment, then resolved. " 'In kind.' You mean by hooking, right?"

"That's what I meant."

"Look, let me tell you one thing, okay? The Angel, she never hook in here, not even for the dentist. She do him, she do him out in the 'burbs, his last appointment for the day. She keep this place outta the fucken life, man. This the best place she ever live, but it still like her tunnel."

"Her tunnel?"

"Yeah. Like in the Nam. The fucken dinks, man, they knew those tunnels were safe. We could chase 'em around all we wanted on top, 'cause we own the air. But they get too pressed, they just drop down a hole and they knew we couldn't get 'em."

He shook his fist at the picture window. "You think living space cost a lot down here, with the harbor and the marketplace and all? Shit, nothing cost more than those tunnels, man. They sweat and they dig and they got little bugs eating them and they die to make them tunnels and make 'em safe, and space was a pre-mi-um item. Most of the fuckers didn't have a change of fucken clothes, man, but they bring what they had into the tunnel."

Niño gulped and talked faster. "Times you go into a tunnel, and you don't hear nothing but you own heart beating, you know it's a cold fucken hole, but you can't take the chance. So you go slow, and maybe you find where they sleep and their shit. Their personal shit, I mean. And it's like maybe one book in dink writing, and a piece of junk jewelry, and a picture. A photo like of their family, all blur 'cause the camera cheap. And all dirty and cracked and mildewed, too, 'cause the tunnel do that to everything. And you hold this fucken photo in you hand, and you sit there like a fucken dummy with you light on it, like you was in a museum staring at the Mona Lisa or something. And you know that fucken dink weigh less than most dogs we got over here and eat a fuck of a lot worse and the only thing that dink fight for is the tunnel you in and the memory he got someplace of the family in that photo that probably got all shot to shit before you even in-country. And you know that dink just like you, man, only he ain't going home after no three hundred sixty-five days. And you hold that fucken photo, and you start to cry. You cry like you was a little baby and mama's tits all dried up, because you hate the little fuckers so much but you see why you ain't gonna beat 'em, not up on top where we trying to fight 'em."

Niño looked hard at me, a look I hadn't seen since I climbed gratefully on the plane that took me back to The World. "Well, this here was Teri's tunnel, man. This was where she hide from the rest of us. And now you gone through her shit and know all about her. And now you gonna find the motherfucken turd who did her, and you gonna tell me, and then I square things all 'round."

He passed his hand over his eyes once, like a jogger wiping off sweat. "I gotta take a piss," he said, hurrying by me into the bathroom and closing the door.

He was in there maybe a minute, water running, when I heard the voice from the alcove. I jumped up, then went on in.

The answering machine, which I'd left running on Play when Niño had called me from the telescope. The tape had almost reached its end. I hit Stop, turned down the volume, and pressed Review. I listened to the tape rewind for only five seconds, when what was recorded had passed. Then I replayed it.

The beginning of the message was gone, probably erased automatically by the recording of messages after it. The only part left was "noon, because I really should like to, uh, see you. Please call, but at the office here. Uh, thanks so much." The incoming tape reached its end, and I turned off the machine.

I walked into the living area near the telescope. If the architect had put in bay windows, I would have been able to look northward, maybe all the way to Swampscott.

* * *

189

"Guess I went a little loco, man."

We were in the elevator riding down, and Niño hadn't spoken since he'd come out of the bathroom.

"Don't worry about it."

He took a deep breath, let it out.

We got off at the lobby level and moved past the guard, who stood with his hands behind his back. He smiled officiously at us.

Outside, Niño said, "You need anything else from me?"

"I don't think so."

He made no effort to walk away. "Man, you been straight with me, I be straight with you."

I thought about the tape, but said, "Go on."

"Staking out you place, I see J.J. and Terdell messing around the cans. Then I spot their tail."

"Tail?"

"Sur-veil-lance. I think about telling you last night, but I want to sleep on it, turn it around a little first. The tail was you classic unmarked sedan. I see it pull in and park while J.J. and Terdell getting ready for you. I was already there, so the tail didn't make me."

"Who was it?"

"Two guys, I didn't try to see closer than that. But one thing sure, they good. Terdell and J.J. grab you, the tail wait till they away to turn on and come out. They follow you, I follow them out to the construction yard."

I considered it. Niño said, "You got to know what I'm thinking."

"Cops."

"That's right. And that mean they see you get snatched and don't feel like doing nothing about it."

"That mean they see me getting beat up, too?"

"Don't think so. I do a little recon before I go into the pipes. The tail just wait outside the construction yard, lights off, like they only care about where J.J.'s car go next and not so much about you."

"Thanks, Niño."

"Yeah, well, I gotta go. Got a major chest-cutting at the Beth Israel, don't you fucken know."

Dr. Rodríguez turned and walked away, pulling out his stethoscope and twirling it like a foot patrolman with a whistle.

NINETEEN

Returning home, I checked my own answering machine. No messages, not even from Chris. I tried his number three times before turning in at midnight. Busy. Or off the hook.

The sun streamed into my bedroom window about 7:00 A.M. I was a lot less stiff and sore than the previous day, so I decided to try a short run. I stretched more slowly and carefully than usual, then went downstairs and out into a beautiful morning.

I jogged gently across Beacon, Bay State Road, and the elevated walkway to the river. The wind was out of the northwest, so I started upstream toward Boston University. I heard a high, whining sound, and looked behind me. Nothing. Then a huge shadow passed over me, too fast for a cloud, too big for a plane. I looked up to see a blimp, all puffy and plump, with absurdly undersized fins and a small, windowed gondola. The whining sound was its engine, a noise like a bus going by you at eighty miles an hour on a highway. The fuselage had a broad green side stripe and the legend FUJI FILM. Its underbelly proclaimed, in smaller letters, OFFICIAL FILM OF MAJOR LEAGUE BASEBALL. As the pilot banked to hover over Fenway Park, I assumed that the abnormally potent Red Sox were going to be featured on Saturday's Game of the Week and wondered why the blimp had to arrive two days early.

Unfortunately, my wondering wasn't distracting me from the ache in my right side. By the time I reached the BU law school tower, the rib cage was screaming at me. I tried cutting my pace, but it was the impact rather than the effort of running that was doing me in. I gritted my teeth and reached the Fairfield footbridge hardly above a walk.

I crossed back over to the city side of Storrow Drive. Stopped at the red light was an old pickup truck with Wisconsin plates and a cranky muffler. Chugging to life and passing me, it displayed a rear bumper sticker reading WOLSKI'S TAVERN: ADVENTURE, DANGER, ROMANCE.

It would be the last laugh of the day.

Holt kept me waiting outside his office for twenty minutes. To reassert control over the situation.

Guinness came out, said, "Now," and sort of held the door for me with his foot. I followed him in.

Holt sat behind his desk, clean pad in front of him. Dawkins lounged at the window, his butt half on and half off the sill. No Murphy. I took a chair across from Holt. Guinness made sure the door closed behind him and then stayed standing at it.

Holt said, "You wanted the meeting, so talk."

"Did Murphy tell you I was contacted by J.J. Braxley yesterday?"

Dawkins said, "He told me. I told the lieutenant here."

"Braxley and I met at J.C. Hillary's under a flag of truce. He's got a step on you guys, because he doesn't think I killed Marsh or Teri Angel. However, he is three-plus pissed at the loss of his product. Seems he extended credit to Marsh at the exchange, and now he doesn't have the money or the drugs."

Holt said, "You tell him to call the Better Business Bureau?"

"He's got his own ideas about consumer protection, Lieutenant. He said if I don't find the stuff, he's going to take it out on Marsh's wife."

Holt and Dawkins just looked at me. I couldn't see Guinness, but I didn't much care what he was doing. I said, "And on his daughter."

Holt said, "Where do they live again?"

He couldn't be serious. "Swampscott. They used to live in Peabody, remember? Then somebody killed the head of the household, and they moved back to the family manor."

Holt said, "Sergeant, where the hell is Swampscott?"

Dawkins said, "Not sure. Somewhere past Everett, I think. Maybe even past Revere."

"Revere! Jesus, I don't think our jurisdiction goes nearly that far, do you, Guinness?"

Guinness said, "Myself, I never been north of Chelsea."

I said, "What the hell is going on here?"

Holt laced his hands behind his head and leaned back. "I don't see where this is any of our concern, geographically speaking."

"What do you mean, 'none of your concern'?"

Dawkins said, "Lieutenant's pretty clear on it,

Cuddy. You said Swampscott, that sound like Essex County to me. Peabody, too."

"And you guys are strictly Suffolk County, right?"

"Right."

I looked at Holt. "You had a double murder here, in your county." I took Dawkins in as well. "And you're after a significant mover of cocaine who operates here." I settled lower into my chair. "So how come nobody's interested in the victim's wife and child being intimidated by a prime suspect in the murder and the clear distributor of the junk?"

Holt said, "First off, Braxley's not a suspect in the murder. Got an alibi four feet thick."

"Second," said Dawkins, "ain't no crimes committed in those other towns linked up with these here."

"How do you figure that?"

"Take Peabody. Nothing happen there except a little animal abuse. The guy done the kitty dead now. Case closed. Swampscott, shit, only action there was you breaking in on Marsh and threatening him."

"I wasn't there, and if I was, I didn't break in."

"And if you did break in, it didn't count, 'cause you had your fingers crossed, right?"

I stopped for a minute and closed my eyes. Holt said, "What do you know? We're boring him as much as he's boring us."

I thought for a moment more, then opened my eyes and looked at him and Dawkins. "You all are going to a hell of a lot of trouble to play keep away with me."

They didn't say anything.

"Long as I have the blindfold on, indulge me a little, okay? I get asked to bodyguard the wife in a divorce case. The husband acts nasty, so I call Murphy, and he calls Dawkins here. Boston Narcotics already knows about Marsh's connection to Braxley, and Murphy

195

passes that on to me, with the warning to stay away from Braxley. Then Marsh dives off the high board, and I get blamed. The case against me has so many holes, you could water the garden with it, but I'm still frozen out of the case, even out of contact with Murphy. Then Braxley and his killer whale come to see me, and maybe thirty minutes after I get away from them, the department's aware of it without my having to file a complaint or anything. Know what I think?"

No response from Holt or even Dawkins, who'd told me to keep quiet about his visit to me that night.

"I think that Narcotics has had Braxley under surveillance for a while. I think that's how come Dawkins knows about Marsh, and Braxley has his solid alibi, and the new centurions all know about me getting worked on before the wounds are closing. And that must mean that Narcotics has a hell of a case it could bring against Braxley. But it's laying back. How come?"

Holt made a sour face; Dawkins smiled.

"Because Braxley is posting up for Narcotics? Not likely. He seems too damned interested in his current business affairs and their continuing vitality to be planning to parachute via some witness protection program. That leaves one other alternative I can see. Narcotics has its sights set on Braxley's supplier, maybe even the supplier's supplier. And the murder of two less-than-model citizens and the potential threat to the family of one of them can be tolerated, at least temporarily, as a cost of the larger drug investigation."

Holt still looked as if indigestion was his main worry. Dawkins brightened his smile a little.

"Well, how am I doing?"

"Brass ring," said Dawkins.

Holt swiveled in his chair. "Goddamn it, Dawkins, who the fuck told you to confirm—"

"Who he gonna tell, Lieutenant? Just the three of us here, and we back each other when we say we deny it. If we ever got to deny it. And chances are we won't."

"Why not?" said Holt.

Dawkins looked over at me and resumed the brighter smile. "'Cause hard charger here gonna find J.J.'s snow and make things all better for the widow and orphan."

"So what do I do?"

Murphy?

"Can't. His hands were tied by me when I asked him to check on a guy just before the guy's killed. Besides, whoever's sitting on Holt would have the juice to sit on Murphy, too. They're peer officers in the chain of command."

Nancy?

"I tied her up, too, as part of my quasi-alibi for the murders. And this surveillance has the smell of something planned and coordinated by people her level never even gets to talk to."

There was a lobster boat, long with the small upright cabin disproportionately forward, plying the harbor below us. I thought the harbor was too polluted to produce edible bottom dwellers, and I made a mental note to lay off seafood for a while.

Does that leave Chris?

"Kind of. He's her attorney. But he won't return my calls."

Can't you see him in person?

"Yeah, but he didn't exactly take the bit in his teeth when Marsh tortured the cat. And J.J. makes Marsh look like an altar boy."

So what are you going to do?

"Go rattle some more cages. If I can find the shooter, I'll find the drugs."

But the only way to help Hanna and Vickie is to give the drugs back to J.J.

"That's the way it shapes up."

Yes, but John, you can't do that.

"I know."

TWENTY
◆

I dialed my answering service from a booth on Broadway. No messages. I tried Chris and drew Eleni, who told me Chris was out but due back after 2:00. I told her it was important that I speak with him and that I would be there at 2:00 sharp. She apologized for his not calling me back the previous evening, but didn't give me any reasons.

I hung up, called Felicia Arnold's office, and waited through receptionist and secretary for her soft, breathy hello.

"Ms. Arnold, John Cuddy."

"I recognized your voice. And please call me Felicia."

"I was hoping I could see you today. Around noon?"

"I believe I can work you in."

"At your office."

"If you insist."

"Ms.—Felicia, please."

"All right. Eleven-thirty?"

"Thank you. See you then."

I got in the Fiat and took Route 1A through Revere, past the Wonderland dog track and the Suffolk Downs horse track. The road breaks over Lynn Beach, then curves north through Swampscott. I found the building again easily, feeling confident that old Bryce would be faithfully manning his computer terminal.

"Oh, Mr. . . . uh, Curry, isn't it?"

He looked insecure, uneasy that I'd walked in on him while his fingers were fondling the keyboard. "Close. Cuddy, John Cuddy."

"Oh, yes, sorry. Names . . ."

"I'm the one who's sorry, Mr. Stansfield, breaking in on you again like this. But I have a few more questions that I thought you might help me with."

"Please, uh, sit down."

"The last time I saw you, I remember your mentioning that Roy Marsh came to work here about the time your uncle died."

"That's right. Well, uh, just after, of course."

"While you were going through your divorce."

"Right."

"Who was your attorney?"

"My . . . uh, for the divorce, you mean?"

"For the divorce."

"I don't quite, uh, see how that's . . ."

"Any of my business?"

"Well, y—no, no. I realize, uh, the police have to look into everything, but . . ."

"I'm not a cop, Mr. Stansfield."

"But you said—"

200

SWAN DIVE

"Only that I was investigating Marsh's death. And I am."

He looked confused. "The police, they, uh, asked me whether I, whether the firm ever hired any Boston private . . . you're, uh, the one they think killed him. Killed Roy!"

"They may have said that, but they don't believe it."

"Well, then, why, uh, should I answer any more of your questions?"

"Because I know about you and Teri Angel."

He was about to say something, but the sound of her name froze his mouth around a syllable like a stop-action photograph.

"Your voice, Mr. Stansfield. Your voice is on her telephone tape machine."

"But, it's been over . . . uh, that is—"

"I haven't told the police."

"You haven't?"

"No. And I hope I won't have to."

He pinched the bridge of his nose. "I don't, uh, understand. I'm sorry."

"One step at a time. Who was your divorce lawyer?"

He tried to focus. "Felicia. Felicia Arnold."

"And through her you met Teri."

"That's correct. My wife and I hadn't . . . uh, for a long time, I was . . . uh, unable."

"And Felicia suggested you see Teri."

"Yes. I didn't know at the time . . . I, uh, know this must sound awfully naive of me, but . . . I, uh, actually thought she was just a sort of . . ."

"Therapist?"

"Yes. I mean, you could tell just hearing her, uh, speak a few sentences that she wasn't educated very formally, but she had a way of listening, of bringing out, uh, things that troubled me. I even tried to pay

201

her the first time by check. And I haven't, uh, hadn't seen her in over a year."

"There's one thing I haven't been able to figure out, Mr. Stansfield. How did Marsh meet Teri?"

"She called here once, to cancel an, uh, appointment I'd made with her, and I was at the post office, so Roy took the call and, uh, asked me who 'Teri' was, so I finally told him after he already guessed."

"He threaten to expose you and her if you didn't set something up for him?"

"Yes. Uh, no, not exactly. I think I, uh, just let him talk to her the next time, over the telephone when she, uh, called here."

And the cops, looking at Teri's or the office phone bills, would just assume it was Teri or Marsh calling the other all along. "Go on."

"Go on? Well, uh, there's not that much more to say."

"I'm afraid there is. What about the drugs?"

"I called, uh, is it Detective Guinness?"

"Yes."

"I called him when those two, uh, Negroes came to see me."

"J.J. and Terdell."

"I don't know their, uh, names, but I was terrified of them. They came to see me and asked where the, uh . . ."

" 'Material'?"

"Yes, where the 'material' was. I, uh, they were quite polite, really, but here, in Swampscott . . . uh, anyway, I told them I didn't have any idea what they were, uh, talking about, and, uh, they left. I immediately called our department here, and, uh, they said to call Boston and speak with Detective Guinness."

"And you told Guinness about it? J.J. and Terdell, I mean."

"Yes."

"I want a look at the files on your insureds."

"I, uh—"

"All the ones that Roy-boy brought into the firm."

"That's not—"

"Which may save me having to tell the police about you and Teri, and them verifying it with—"

"All right, Mr. Cuddy. All right. I, uh, scare quite easily enough. You can stop there."

The look on his face made me sorry I'd played so cute toward the end. He turned away from me and toward the keyboard, tapping, pausing, and tapping again. "Can you scroll?"

I stood and moved behind him. "Why don't you do it. I don't want to mess anything up, and I'm sure you'd be faster than I would."

He straightened and steadied a little bit at my compliment. "Here come the A's."

Over his shoulder, I watched the screen for twenty minutes. A lot of people buying a lot of arcane coverages. A few names you'd recognize from the newspaper, mainly the sports, business, and government sections. Both my lawyers were telling the truth. Felicia was a big customer, Chris didn't appear at all.

She unfolded sinuously from her desk chair. Someone once told me that grace is the movement of weight in balance. It suited her perfectly.

She said, "I wondered if our last discussion would have put you off?"

I closed the door behind me and took her outstretched hand, getting close enough to notice she was wearing a little more perfume than usual. Not crass or cloying, just a faint enhancement. When the fish doesn't bite, sweeten the bait.

I let go of her hand a trifle sooner than she would

have and dropped into the client chair without answering her question. She stayed standing and looked down at me.

"You know, you really are an intriguing man."

"Thanks."

"No, truly. I've seen more than most, and you really are here because of what you're working on, not because you want some action. This Marsh matter is the cause of, not the excuse for, your continuing interest in me."

"That's right."

She poured herself back into the chair. "I find that exciting, you know? Not being the central figure for a change."

"I have a few—"

"Let's go to bed, you and I."

I stopped, she arched an eyebrow and smiled.

"I'd regret it," I said.

"That depends on whether you say yes or no."

I didn't respond; she went on. "You see, if you say yes, the earliest you can regret it is tomorrow morning."

"You're probably overestimating me."

"Whereas, if you say no, you'll begin regretting it immediately."

"Sounds like I get depressed either way."

The eyebrow came down, the smile slid into a disgusted frown, and she said, "I'm not sure I will have time to see you today after all."

"What if it's talk to me or talk to the cops?"

She laughed, regaining ground. "Please, don't threaten me about the killings. I'm a lawyer, remember? We invented threats."

"Actually, I wasn't thinking so much about the killings as about the hookers and the drugs."

She finished the laugh, but smoothly, as if it hadn't

died in her throat. She leaned back with a "Boy, I've got you now" look. The best trial lawyer from my days at Empire used to say that was the look he'd put on when the opposition had just harpooned him in front of the jury.

"The hookers, you say?"

"Yeah, like Teri Angel in Boston."

"The poor girl killed with Marsh?"

"That's her."

"Are you suggesting I knew her?"

"Uh, yes, I'm afraid, uh, I am."

Felicia's face indicated she didn't like my imitation. Not even a little.

I said, "Marsh met Teri through Stansfield, and Stansfield met Teri through you."

"I don't know what you're talking about."

"The vagaries of memory. I'm sure the probate court appearance docket and Teri's phone bills will refresh yours when the time comes. We could probably even find some folks at the Barry who could prove you knew her socially, too, but for now, let's try the drugs. Remember them?"

Her eyes were glittering, but the voice was still steady. "I thought the police hadn't found the drugs Marsh was supposed to have had with him."

"Let's say they haven't. Let's also say that the stuff hasn't shown up on the street."

"It would be hard to tell if it had, you know. One package of it is pretty much the same as another."

"According to my sources, this package is distinctive and it isn't being pushed."

"And therefore?"

"And therefore, we find ourselves in something of an illogical situation."

"How so?"

"Somebody mugs me, uses my gun to rip off Marsh

and kill Teri Angel, yet the drugs aren't being marketed."

She looked at me. I said, "Any ideas?"

"No."

"Oh, Ms. Arnold. Not very lawyerly of you. One thought certainly comes to my mind."

She just kept looking. I said, "How about a little home consumption?"

"I don't know what you're talking about."

"Well, let me spin it out a bit. Marsh is a distributor for Braxley Cocaine Incorporated, okay? Old Roy has the perfect cover for visiting a lot of people each week. So to make him look plausible, his customers buy bushels of insurance, coverage they don't need and never claim on. That means they pay a premium to the insurance company over and above the cost of the junk, but hell, that's a small price to avoid the inconvenience of driving into the seedier areas of our metropolitan area to score a few lines. Marsh makes out on both ends of the deal, the drug margin and his insurance commissions. But Roy is a greedy kind of guy, angry at a nickel because it isn't a dime, you know?"

"Picturesque, but a trifle tedious."

"We'll cut to the punch line, then. You turn out to be one of his insurance customers. You don't strike me as a heavy user, but Paulie-boy's so stoked he's got to wear shades to brush his teeth. Maybe the drug connection is your way of keeping pocket stallions like him in the stable."

"You contemptible—"

"Then something goes wrong, and maybe Marsh starts thinking what I'm thinking."

"Do you realize the potential liability you're incurring?"

"I'm judgment-proof. Prove what you want, there's

no pot of gold at the end of this rainbow. Anyway, Marsh starts thinking that a blue-chip lawyer like you might pay to protect her license from embarrassing probes about drugs and hookers."

"And so Marsh starts blackmailing me?"

"It would explain how a schmuck like Roy could get a lawyer like you for his divorce case. It would also explain how you might know when Marsh saw Teri Angel at the Barry."

"I'm really disappointed in you, Cuddy. Even though I'm an established attorney, you just subconsciously assume that since I'm a woman, too, I'd either have to accept whatever Marsh tried to pull or set up the clumsy frame you claim you're in with the police. Well, look around you. I've worked a lot of years to build up what I've got here, and I'm not about to give it away." She hit a button on her phone and barked "Paul!" into it.

The door to the adjoining office flew open and Troller burst into the room. He was wearing suit pants, a long-sleeved oxford shirt, sleeves rolled up, and a handsome regimental tie. He grinned at me and started bouncing on the balls of his feet and shaking out his shoulders.

"I think Paul's been looking forward to this, Cuddy."

American-trained boxers have two major strengths. They are used to dishing out punishment until the other guy falls, so you have a tough time coming back against them once they get in the first licks. They're used to taking punishment, too. In Saigon, I remember seeing a good MP stunned to find that a nightstick to the collarbone wouldn't stop a welterweight with a few drinks in him.

Boxers have a weakness, too, however. They tend to think they're invincible in close. Even wearing a tie.

SWAN DIVE

I gambled Paulie's first punch would be a feint. He
jabbed with his left at my eye, then pulled it short,
instead driving a good right up and into my body. I
caved, keeping my elbows and hands tight to protect
the ribs and face. He followed with a left to the body,
stepping forward to really bury it. I folded so that
most of his force was spent in the air, leaving him near
enough for me to grab his tie. I yanked the shorter end
down with my right hand, my left forcing the knot
high and hard into his throat. His face bulged, both
his hands scrabbling to the front of his collar. I let go
of the knot, clamping both my hands on the insides of
his wrists and pulling his hands apart to benediction
width. I had a feeling my grip would outlast his air.

Arnold probably couldn't tell what I'd done, but as
Paul and I danced around, she could see that he wasn't
getting the best of it. She let it go on for a while, Paul's
face and motions growing more grotesque by the
moment. He started to buckle at the knees, and she
said sharply. "Enough, Cuddy, enough!"

I let him go, and he wobbled down, enough consciousness left to allow him to loosen his own tie. He
wrenched in fitful breaths, an asthmatic at a flower
show.

She said, "That wasn't pretty."

"Neither is what Braxley'll do to Hanna and Vickie
if he doesn't get his drugs back. I don't want them hurt
anymore from all this, but I can't guard their house
twenty-four hours a day. That leaves me with
Braxley's drugs as the lesser of two evils, Ms. Arnold,
and if you can help out with that, you'd best do it
soon."

Troller wheezed out some words. "Chris . . . tides
. . . is her lawyer . . . Go talk to the . . . bastard."

"I wouldn't be bad-mouthing your alibi, Paulie-
boy."

Arnold said, "What do you mean?"

"Christides told me he saw the Great White Hope there at some lawyer dinner up here while I was being slugged down in Boston."

Troller pulled himself into a chair. "He's lying."

I turned to look at him. "What?"

Troller worked his head around on his neck and swallowed like a kid taking castor oil. "The dinner . . . got wrecked. Fire alarm . . . Barely had drinks before . . . everybody had to get out . . . Christides didn't come back in for dinner."

"What time was this?"

"What?"

"When the fire alarm went off."

"Don't know . . . The president . . . started some long-winded welcome . . . maybe six-fifteen, six-thirty."

Arnold said, "What difference does that make, Cuddy? You told me you were hit a little after five."

I looked from one to the other. "I don't know."

TWENTY-ONE

By the time I walked to my car, the adrenaline from dealing with Troller was fading, hunger rapidly replacing it. I settled for a touristy place on the harbor and had a mediocre burger with great french fries and two frosty drafts.

I pulled up at the curb in front of Chris's house at 1:45. His old Pontiac was parked at an angle in the double driveway, almost a warning to potential clients not to bother knocking on the office door. I pushed into the reception area.

Cousin Fotis nearly drew down on me, reluctantly bringing an empty hand out from under his jacket and newspaper. He said, "Office closed today."

"Chris is expecting me."

He was trying to decide what to make of that when Nikos appeared in the connecting doorway to the house proper. The new arrival muttered something in Greek.

Fotis said to me, "Eleni say to wait here. He come."

I sat down, and Nikos disappeared into the house. I watched my friend read his paper for about five minutes before Chris nervously bustled through the doorway and headed straight for his inner office.

"Jeez, I'm sorry about not getting back to you, John, but I been swamped here."

I swung my head slowly, taking in the empty office. "I can see it."

Chris didn't react to the sarcasm. "So, what's up?"

"You heard from Hanna recently?"

"Hanna?"

"Yeah, Hanna Marsh. Remember, the widow of the guy I'm supposed to have killed?"

"C'mon, John, don't start foaming at the mouth, huh? I told you, I been up to my—"

"Look, Chris, cut the shit, okay? I've been kind of up to my ears in this, too. We've got a major problem."

He moved his lips around a little, then said, "This guy Braxley?"

"This guy Braxley."

"Christ, John, he caught up with me yesterday."

"He did?"

"Yeah, coming out of court. I park in the lot around the corner, two bucks cheaper, you know? Anyway, this guy Braxley and some other one smells like a rendering plant grab me, nobody else around, nobody's ever around when you need them. They say Marsh had these drugs on him and now they're gone and what did I think was going to happen to the guy who's got them. They scared the shit out of me."

"Chris, they *beat* the shit out of me. And now they're threatening Hanna and Vickie. And you know what? I can't even get Hanna's lawyer to return my phone calls."

"John, I said I was sorry about that. Eleni . . ."

I lowered my voice. "Eleni?"

"It's the MS, the sclerosis, you know? She has the good days and the bad. Lately, it's been mostly bad."

I thought she'd sounded fine on the telephone each time, but I said, "All right. We've all been under a lot of pressure here. But it's up to you and me to cover Hanna."

"You and me? What about the police?"

"The Boston cops are after bigger fish than Braxley. They've got reason to want him on the street for a while, not away in a cell somewhere. They're playing down the killings until they make the bigger score."

"Jeez, I never . . . what about Swampscott?"

"You know anybody there?"

"On the force, you mean?"

"On the force, in the politics, in the PTA, for God's sake. Anybody who might care what Braxley would do to Hanna and Vickie."

Chris flinched. "Nobody, John. I don't really deal in those kinda circles much, you know?"

"Terrific."

"How . . . how long before this Braxley stops talking and starts doing other things?"

"I don't know. He's thrown scares into a lot of people, but as far as I know, I'm the only one he's roughed up. My guess is that he's going to give me a little more time to try to solve things for him, but I'd hate to bet on it."

"I don't know what to tell you, John. The system, it don't deal too well with crud like this Braxley."

"Or Marsh."

"Right, right. Or him too. It works pretty good ninety, ninety-five percent of the time. But something like this . . ."

"What about the courts?"

212

"Aw, John, what courts? The probate court, the family court, there's no more husband so there's no more divorce. Sure as hell no jurisdiction over some drug dealer from the city. Plus, like you say, he hasn't really done anything criminal yet."

"He broke into Marsh's house, ransacked it."

"Which probably wasn't reported over there by anybody, right? Not the nurse, not Hanna, nobody."

"So where does that leave us?"

"I don't know. We can't get him locked up for what he's thinking, you know."

"He said he was going to force Hanna to sell the house to cover the drugs if he didn't get them back."

"Look, John. He tells her that, she decides to sell, she sells, she gives him the money, what am I supposed to do, huh?"

"Oh, Chris, for chrissake, that's duress. There's got to be something you can do."

"John, John. I gotta admit, it sounds bad to a layman like you, but she'd have to resist the sale, and then she risks Vickie getting hurt. Or she goes through with the sale and won't give him the money. Guys like this Braxley, they got long memories, John. And even longer arms, get me?"

"Meaning he waits till the heat's off, then settles things."

"Right. Even if she sells and skips, guy like Braxley's got contacts lotsa places. One of them sooner or later gets to her."

"Unless the cops make their big move first."

"Which you say they ain't about to do. Think about it, John. The cops are willing to let two killings go by for a while, must be something big enough to carry another couple for the ride."

Which was what I'd told Holt and Dawkins myself. I wriggled in the uncomfortable old wooden chair.

"John, I don't wanna seem rude or nothin', but I really gotta—"

"Chris, you said you saw Paul Troller at the lawyer's dinner the night I got hit."

He frowned at me. "That's right, I did. What's that got to do with this here?"

"Troller says there was a fire. Or at least an alarm pulled. The dinner got screwed up."

"So?"

"So why didn't you tell me that?"

Chris shook his head, then dipped his face once into his hands, like a bucket into a well. "Jeez, John, I don't know what's the matter with you. You brought up this Troller like he coulda been the one to sap you, right?"

"That's right."

"Okay, so I saw him before we sat down for the dinner when it couldn't have been him that hit you. Five, five-fifteen, something, right?"

"Right."

"Okay, so I don't see what the hell difference it makes whether he stayed for the dinner or not. I just didn't think to mention it to you."

"He says he did stay. He says you didn't."

"I can't tell you whether he stayed or not, because personally I couldn't give a shit. But he's right as fucken rain about me not staying. Jeez, the only thing goes on longer than the speeches at that kinda thing is the Arctic winter, you know?"

"So where did you go?"

"Here. Home. I was worried about Eleni, remember?"

"Why?"

Chris started to turn bright red and rose out of his chair. "Why? Why, you stupid shit, because you were playing Charles fucken Bronson with Marsh in his

214

shower, that's why! Remember that? Remember why I fucken asked you as a favor, as a friend, to bodyguard at a simple little divorce conference that turns into fucken Armageddon? The guy scared me, John, you happy you got me to say that again? He scared me, and now this Braxley fucken terrifies me, and I'm getting . . ." He suddenly seemed to just run out of steam, dumping his body back into the seat. "John, why don't you get the fuck out of here, okay? Leave me alone, just leave me with my problems for a while."

I got up and walked past Fotis, who was grinning behind his paper just about enough to set me off.

I headed the car back toward 128 South. I had some questions for Hanna that I couldn't ask over the telephone, but I wanted to think things through first. I got onto Route 1 and sat for nearly an hour with four hundred other cars before the state police permitted us, one at a time, to crawl around a jackknifed double-trailered tank truck that was oozing God knows what into a ditch on the side of the road.

I stopped at the office, paid some bills, and perfunctorily worked on two other matters I'd been pursuing.

I reconsidered a call I'd been mulling in the traffic jam, then dialed it anyway.

"Nancy Meagher."

"Nancy, it's John. John Cuddy."

She laughed. "You think I know so many Johns I can't place your voice?"

I thought back to how similarly Felicia Arnold responded in our telephone conversation. Maybe it's the law school training.

"John, are you still there?"

"Yes, sorry. Nance, I need the answers to a few questions about attorney licensing."

"John, if it's about the Marsh case, you know I can't talk."

"I know. It's more general than that. Say a lawyer was caught doing drugs, cocaine. What would happen?"

"Caught? You mean by the police?"

"Or an informer. Somebody who goes to the cops or the bar authorities with ironclad evidence that the lawyer was buying substantial amounts."

"Well, putting aside the criminal proceedings, the Board of Bar Overseers would probably start an investigation through its lawyer staff, with a hearing and all before the board."

"What then?"

"Then, if the evidence is persuasive, the board seeks sanctions, with a single justice of the Supreme Judicial Court eventually ruling on what was to happen as a penalty. Of course, sometimes I think the board just lets the criminal side run its course, and then nails the lawyer involved pretty quickly if a guilty verdict comes down. It saves double effort that way."

"Would the substantial buying of cocaine be grounds for disbarment?"

"Oh, I would think so. Usually it's more white-collar stuff, like tax evasion or real estate fraud, but I've never researched it. Why?"

"Last question. Would they also boot a lawyer who referred divorce clients to prostitutes for 'sex therapy'?"

"John, have you been drinking?"

"On the level."

"God, John, I don't know. The prosecutor in me says yes, but the way things are today, maybe not. A neutral lawyer could probably think of at least a couple of reasons why that should be handled a little quieter."

"Thanks. Look, I want to see you again, but with all of this . . ."

"I've waited this long, John. But pretty soon I'm going to need more from you."

We hung up. I called the number Niño had given me. A woman who might have been Salomé, the tougher, older one at lunch, answered and then put Niño on. He was pleased to hear my voice and was still very interested in receiving any "mer-chan-dise" I might uncover.

Next I called Braxley and asked him if the "material" had hit the street yet. He said no. He also said he hoped I was making progress on the material, because he had heard that the real estate market was rising, making the near future a "very excellent" time to sell.

I put the receiver back in its cradle and rotated my chair to look out over the Common. Whoever kills Marsh and Teri takes the drugs, but doesn't try to sell them. Because the killer is using them personally, like Felicia. Or because the killer wanted Marsh, or Teri, or both, dead and didn't give a damn about the drugs, like Hanna. But why does anybody go to the trouble of framing me first?

I got up, locked up, and drove home. Nobody was waiting for me anywhere. I had a pizza delivered, washed it down with my last three Molson Goldens, and went to sleep at 10:00 P.M.

TWENTY-TWO

I drove past the Swampscott house twice, but saw no sign of Braxley or Terdell for half a mile in either direction. Assuming they weren't anchored offshore in a Boston whaler, I backed into her driveway alongside the apparently fixed Escort and got out of my car. I rang the bell, then knocked just as Hanna opened the door. She had a towel in her hand.

"John."

"Hanna, I wonder if I could talk with you for a while?"

"Oh, of course, of course. Come in."

She led me into the living room. It now looked straightened, restored. Hanna said, "I remember you don't like the coffee, but could we sit in the kitchen? I'm doing the laundry, and Vickie is in the yard with Rocky. I want to keep the eye on her. Like you said?"

"The kitchen would be fine."

I sat on a stool, Hanna folding linens from a plastic basket and turned three-quarters away from me so she could see the child through the window. Vickie had a furry beanbag of some kind on a piece of cord, and would swing it out toward a low hanging bush, then work it back to herself like a fly-caster after trout. The quarry was the kitten, who would pounce on the bag from beneath the bush, tussle with it wildly, then bound back under cover to await the next toss.

I said, "She looks happy."

Hanna smiled. "She is. To be home, with her new kitty. And I am happy."

"To be home?"

The smile turned wistful. "To be home, and to be free of Roy, that too, I think." She creased a pillowcase precisely, like a marine furling the colors at sunset.

"Hanna—"

"I bury him yesterday."

"I'm sorry?"

"Roy. I bury him yesterday."

I couldn't read any emotion at all from her. "How did Vickie take it?"

"I did not have Vickie there. They tell me it is cheaper to do the cremation, but I tell them, no, I want him buried. I tell the BMW man, 'Come get your car, I make no more payments on it.' He was mad, so was the boat man, I call and say, 'Come, take back your boat, no more payments on that either.'" She shook her head. "They both say they sue me, but I need the money so I can bury Roy. And I bury him so I can go back if things ever get bad again, go back and stand at his grave and remember what bad really is."

I waited till I was sure she was finished. Then I said, "Have you seen Braxley again? Or heard from him?"

219

"No."

"Hanna, I met with the police. And with Chris." I summarized for her what I'd learned from each.

She listened, politely but still without emotion. "Was that different from what you expect them to say?"

"No."

She shrugged. "So I wait, right? For the drugs to be found or Braxley to come see me again."

When I didn't answer, she said, softly, "It doesn't matter. It is still better than Roy."

"Hanna, I'm at a dead end looking for the drugs. You told me the last time that you didn't really know anything about them, and I believe you. But if you can think of anything that would help, I'd appreciate it."

She gestured with a dish towel. "When I come back here, I pull the things together that the drug people pull apart. I don't know Roy's life since I leave him so well, but the only things I can see gone that I remember are a suitcase and the video things."

"When you say video things, you mean the camera and the case for it?"

"Yes, the case he carry the drugs in. And the stand thing."

"The tripod?"

"Yes. Tripod."

I thought back to Maylene's comment at lunch about Teri's supposed screen test. "Did Roy take the camera and tripod out of the house much?"

Hanna dropped her eyes. "Sometimes."

"What for?"

She blushed. "You need to know this?"

"Hanna, I don't know what I need to know."

She abandoned the laundry and hugged herself as though she were chilly, staring out at Vickie and away from me. "Roy, he like to . . . use the camera when

220

we . . . in our bedroom. He set up the tripod thing and the camera and then . . . take the pictures of us . . . of him more, doing the things to me. He put all the lights on and buy some kind of film you don't need special lights for. Then he . . . take the pictures and watch them on the TV." She cleared her throat. "Enough?"

I wished it were. "One more question?"

She nodded without turning to me.

"You said he used to take the video things out of the house. Do you know why?"

Hanna ground her teeth, but spoke evenly. "When he thought I wasn't doing . . . it right, he would yell at me, hit me. Then he wouldn't want me for . . . till the marks go away. So he take the things and go see the girl."

"The girl who was killed."

"Yes. He tell me he going to see her, then he go with the things, go to her, then he come back with them, the pictures, and he . . . put them on the TV and make me watch, watch him and her to make me do better for him."

I couldn't think of anything else to say except "I'm sorry."

She waved a hand at me, the tears beginning to flow. I got up and left her.

I drove west to Route 1, then took it north to I-95. I swung off onto 495 and then exited at Tullbury, stopping at the first public phone I saw. There was only one "Leo Kelley" with an "ey" in the book. I dialed, heard Sheilah's voice answer, and hung up. Ten minutes later, I was outside her father's place, his red Buick gleaming in the driveway.

The house was a mini-Victorian. A disproportionate wraparound porch held heavy, old-fashioned wicker furniture. The white paint on the chairs was bright and fresh, but the cushions were dirty and flat. I pictured Leo thinking that he had kept up his side of the maintenance but his dead wife had failed in her attention to the needlework. I knocked on the screen door and heard two voices say "I'll get it." Sheilah arrived first, stopping short when she saw me and causing her father to bump into her from behind.

"Christ, Sheilah, what the hell did—" Leo Kelley became aware of me and changed to "Not you again!"

Sheilah said, "What do you want this time?"

"Goddamn it, it don't matter what he wants. This is my town, and I'm gonna call Tommy down to the station and get—"

"Dad, please? Okay?"

"I don't know what you—"

"Dad!"

"Awright, fine. Fine! I wash my hands of it. You wanna act like a two-year-old, fine. Go off with this guy now. Or the jig drug pusher. I don't care. Just keep 'em out of my house and out of my life, okay?" He stomped back into the house somewhere.

She looked at me. "Well?"

"Your father didn't say anything about the porch."

She tried to make up her mind, then unlatched the screen door and came out. She was wearing jeans a size too large for fashion and a nondescript short-sleeved shirt that was poorly cut. She plunked herself down in one of the chairs and crossed her legs, foot jiggling nervously. I sat on the railing.

"Ms. Kelley, have you seen Braxley or his friends?"

"No, and I don't want to, either. Which is why I'm talking to you."

Her logic escaped me. "I want to ask you some questions about Roy Marsh and his video equipment."

A little blood drained from her face. "Go ahead."

"You and I talked at the house in Swampscott after it was searched. You said the only thing you noticed missing was the videocamera and its case."

"Uh-huh."

"Was the tripod gone, too?"

She worked her mouth, but just said, "Yes."

"After I left, did you notice anything else missing?"

"No."

"How about Roy's suitcase?"

"No. I mean, I don't know. He had a bunch of them, I didn't really pay any attention, you know?"

"So one of the suitcases could have been missing too?"

"Yeah, could have been. I was upset, you saw me."

"You said the last time you saw Roy was Sunday night into Monday morning, about one A.M., right?"

"When I got home from work."

"Before the house was ransacked."

"Before . . . yeah, of course before. They didn't search the place till . . ."

"Till after Roy was dead?"

"Yeah." She recrossed her legs, still twitching the dangling foot.

"You also said you spent the day, Monday, doing errands and so forth, since it was your day off. You didn't see Roy at all."

"Right, right. He was up and gone before I was. Like I told you."

"And then you came here, to your Dad's for dinner."

She chafed. "Right. Look, I've got to be in to work by three-thirty and I got a lot of things to do first, so if—"

"Roy had the camera rolling when you and he made love, didn't he?"

She jerked, like a dog on a short leash.

I said, "The video equipment. Roy had it set up in the bedroom of the house in Swampscott so he could tape you and him together."

She remembered to breathe, but she had to try hard to get everything else started again. "You didn't . . . you didn't look at the tapes . . ."

"No, Ms. Kelley. I didn't and I wouldn't. Hopefully, nobody else will either. Provided you confirm some things."

She looked absent now, away from it all. "Things."

"The video equipment, the camera and tripod and all, it was gone Monday morning when you woke up, right?"

"No."

"No?"

She shook her head to make me understand. "No, no. It was . . . it was gone when I got home from the errands. I went upstairs to take a shower and saw it was gone. We'd . . . he'd had it set up on Sunday morning in the bedroom and it was gone. I just thought . . ."

"That Roy had gone to see Teri Angel again?"

"Whatever her name was."

"According to one of Teri's friends, Roy was with Teri on Saturday night. He was with you Sunday morning and night, then back again with Teri on Monday night?"

She lifted a hand, covering her eyes. "Look, Roy liked . . . he had a lot of sexual energy. And demands."

"When you saw Roy on Sunday night, he asked you to stay at the house in Swampscott on Monday, didn't he?"

Sheilah didn't answer.

"He asked you to be there so he could have an alibi, like on Friday afternoon with the cat."

"You don't understand . . . what I was going through. I loved him, and I didn't want to believe what you said to me at the hospital, about him doing that to her cat and threatening his wife and the girl. So I asked him, and he . . . he hit me, telling me if I really loved him, I'd trust him on something that bad. That's when I knew for sure he'd hurt the cat. When he told me I should be trusting him."

"Then he asked you again to cover for him Monday night?"

"Yes, but he didn't say why and I wasn't about to ask him after the 'trust' thing, so I told him I'd be there and then I couldn't, just couldn't, I mean, what if it was going to be his wife this time, or the little girl? So I called my dad and came up here, then kept trying to call Roy, and not getting any answer, then I got worried and I drove back down there and the phone rang, the police . . ."

She seemed to stall and glide to a stop. She didn't cry, she just sat there, elbow on crossed knee, face buried in upturned palm.

"Ms. Kelley?"

She stayed put.

"Ms. Kelley?"

No reaction at all. I got up, thinking at least I'd have to be facing only one more woman Roy Marsh had wrecked.

Stopping at a greasy spoon that looked like a failed Dairy Queen, I ordered lunch. I also ran over what I had.

Sheilah Kelley's admission about the camera and tripod being gone before Marsh was killed made everything else come together. I'd been assuming all along that whoever mugged me also murdered Roy and Teri, and no one fit as the framer. That was because only one person had the nerve and the attitude to set me up. Roy himself.

Marsh has a bad day Friday, Hanna demanding the house, me visiting him in the shower. Not exactly a choirboy, he still doesn't dare target Hanna or Vickie, especially after the cat episode. So he decides the best way to come out ahead is to blackmail Felicia, who wasn't able to head Hanna off on the house. But Felicia's too smart to be tied into the drug buying in a traceable way, so he needs concrete evidence of something else unworthy. From Stansfield, Marsh knows Felicia refers clients to Teri. Maybe not grounds for disbarment, but enough leverage to pry the price of the house from Felicia. Then on Saturday night, Teri says something that makes Roy realize that Felicia is also one of Teri's crossover freelancers and that Felicia's next due to see her on Monday night. That gives Roy all of Sunday and Monday to plan.

Roy comes to Boston to mug me for the gun and have me as a fall guy if something goes wrong at the Barry. But then old Roy somehow botches the camera/gun confrontation with Felicia and Teri. Felicia grabs the video stuff and the drugs and takes off, leaving me center stage in Roy's bungled frame.

It all made sense if I could prove Felicia knew Teri. Stansfield and probably other divorce clients would do, even if Patch might not recognize Felicia as one of Teri's regulars. And Felicia had a very deep pocket, plenty enough to pay off J.J. and get Hanna off the hook.

Feeling optimistic for the first time in four days, I finished my meatball sub and soggy potato chips. Then I used the outside booth to call my answering service. There was a message from Ed, my friend at the South Boston courthouse. Now that I had Stansfield tying Felicia to Teri, I really didn't need Ed's help anymore. However, he must have jumped through hoops to get the information for me that quickly, so I called him back.

"Clerk's Office."

"Ed?"

"Ed? No, I think . . . just a second." The voice yelled off the line. "Hey, Charley? Charley! Hey, you seen Ed? Yeah, that's what I thought." He came back to me, conversationally. "Yeah, it's like I thought. Ed's covering the second session, might be there all—hold it, he's coming through the door now. Hey, Ed?"

There was a clunking noise, then, "Hell-o."

"Ed, John Cuddy."

"Ah, oh, yes, Lieutenant, that file just came in. Hold on, will you?"

"Thanks, Ed."

About twenty seconds passed. "Lieutenant?"

"Right here."

"Yeah, I got this so quick 'cause I knew you really needed it. We don't have no Federal fucking Express on these, you know?"

"How does dinner at Amrheins strike you?"

"That should just about cover the postage, all right. I got your 'Papangelis, Theresa A.' right in front of me here. Now, what do you want?"

"Charge and date?"

"Soliciting, November of seventy-eight. Knocked down to a disorderly, she agreed to facts sufficient."

"Meaning the lawyer basically got her off on the soliciting charge in exchange for her admitting there

227

were facts sufficient to find her guilty of disorderly conduct?"

"That's how I'd read it. Anything else?"

"Yeah, who've they got as her lawyer?"

"Oh, right. Just a second . . . Yeah, here it is."

Ed told me, and the sky began to fall.

TWENTY-THREE

The Pontiac looked more rusted, the converted garage more shoddy. I opened the door without knocking, but there was no cousin in the waiting area. Chris sat at the secretary's desk, efficiently hunting and pecking at a form in the typewriter and looking up in embarrassment when he saw it was me.

"Jeez, John, this temp service, I gotta change—"

"I know, Chris."

"About the temp place?"

"No. About Marsh, Teri, everything."

His eyes went out of focus. Standing shakily, he said, "Maybe we better . . . the office."

I didn't have to ask him to start at the beginning.

"It was the MS, John, swear to God it was. Don't let nobody kid you, you can't fight something like that. Before, Eleni and I were doing okay, hell, I was doing better than okay in the office by the courthouse there.

Then the MS hit her, and it all, I don't know, just dribbled away. The money, the clients, her and me."

"You represented Teri back in 1978, a long time before the MS."

"Huh? Oh, yeah, I did, but I didn't start . . . start going to see her then. That was just how I met her, doing a courtesy thing for somebody up where she lived. Just like I got involved with that fucking Marsh, helping somebody out."

"When did you first start seeing Teri?"

"Maybe a year ago. I had this closing in Boston, at three. The lawyers down there, they think everybody's in a big-time firm, you know? They schedule everything figuring that the guy on the other side's just gonna catch the five-ten for Wellesley. Or maybe is gonna go back to his State Street office and put in another five hours before calling it a day. You come in like I have to, though, that Route One's a nightmare anywhere from four to seven going north out of the city. So I finished up with the closing at like four-fifteen and walked over to the Parker House. Have a few drinks, wait out the traffic, you know?"

"I know. And Teri was there?"

"Yeah. Oh, not hooking or anything, the Parker House'd never stand for that. No, she was just having a drink at the bar, and some salesman with a garment bag under his stool was kind of hitting on her, and she sees me and drops him to come over and say hi." Chris took a deep breath. "Christ, John, you shoulda seen her. Beautiful, like somebody's dream of what a woman should look like. The legs, not like . . . anyway, we started talking and drinking and I lost track of the time, and next thing I know we're in the Barry, and then all I know is that I feel like a man. For the first time in years, I feel like a fucking god."

"You kept on seeing her after that?"

"Yeah. Once, maybe twice a month. Always down there."

"Even at that, must have gotten kind of expensive."

"Oh, no. She wouldn't . . . look, I didn't have any stars in my eyes or nothing. I knew what she was doing for a living. But since I had helped that once, when she didn't know her way around, she . . . she saw me for free. Her pimp didn't care what she did free-lance, and Teri knew about Eleni, the MS and all."

"That night. I've got a pretty good idea what happened, but I'd like to hear it from you."

Chris tilted forward in the chair, working his hands like a man lathering with washroom liquid soap. "I went to the bar association social, but with things not going so good for me, professionally speaking, I figured the cocktail time would be a better chance for getting some business than the dinner itself. You know, happy hour, you can move around, work the room a little, but at dinner, you're stuck with whoever's next to you or across the table. So, I was going to duck out after the drinks anyway, the fire alarm thing just gave me the perfect excuse for leaving."

"You were planning to meet Teri that night?"

"Yeah, she even called me here, which she never did, called me from somewheres, insistent-like that I be there and on time. That she wanted to . . . wanted to try something different. So I got there all right, on time."

"You knew the room number?"

"Teri had some kind of arrangement with the hotel. I never asked, nobody there knew me from Adam and I wanted to keep it that way. But she was always in the same room, with the good view."

"What happened?"

"I knocked, she opened up, she was wearing . . .

231

one of those teddy things, you know? All lace and black and see-through. Usually, we'd have a drink, talk a little first. This time, she wants me to come right over to the bed, maybe five feet from the closet there. The Barry, it's so old, they still got real closets you can walk into, and the door's open maybe three inches. Well, she's got some kind of Walkman thing she wants me to put on. I think it's screwy, but she'd said she wanted to try something different, so I went along. It was like piano and lute or something, just continuous instrumental shit."

"To cover any background noise you might have heard."

Chris looked down. "That hit me later. Anyway, she puts these earphones on me, has me hold the little tape thing, and she undresses me. Slowly, kissing me and rubbing against me, everywhere, with everything. Then she . . . she takes me into her mouth, and goes wild on me. Jeez, John, all the other times with her, she never did anything that made me feel like that. I was saying things, I don't know what I was saying, but every time I'd go to turn, or try to touch her, she'd nudge me back, sort of sideways to the closet."

"For the camera angle."

Chris just continued. "As I'm . . . getting ready to finish, the closet door bangs open and there's Marsh, dressed in nothing but skivvies and some kinda doctors' gloves. I can see a camera on a tripod thing behind him, and he's smiling and holding a gun on me. I thought I was gonna shit."

"What happened then?"

"Teri jumps up and starts screaming at him. Something like, 'What the fuck's wrong with you? You're fucking up my screen test.' He's moving around the bed toward the window, kind of getting away from her but also kind of . . . I know this sounds weird, John, but kind of like he was trying to look at everything from a different angle, like he was trying to figure out if he shoulda had the camera somewheres else."

"Go on."

"Well, I didn't know what to think. I mean, my brain's just about dead. Then he waves the gun at me and says to get down on the floor, at the foot of the bed. On all fours, like . . . like some kind of animal. So I do, trying to figure out what I'm supposed to do, what the fuck is going on."

"What's Teri doing all this time?"

"She's still screaming at him. He yells back. 'This fuckhead wants my house. Well, he ain't gonna get it. What he's gonna get is sorry he ever tried to fuck with me. How do you suppose his wife will like your debut?' That's the word he used, too, 'debut,' like he'd thought all this through and planned out his speech."

"What did Teri say to that?"

"She went crazy. She said something like, 'You bastard! You didn't say nothing about that. You just said we needed an ordinary guy for the porn people.' Marsh says to her, 'You stupid cunt, you'd believe rain ain't wet.'"

"Then what?"

"Then . . ." Chris dropped his head till all that kept his jaw from his chest were the chins underneath. "Then she said, 'Well, you ain't doing this with me,' all defiant-like, then she stomped up and across the bed, and made to go in the closet, like after the camera. And Marsh, that, that . . . pig says, 'Even better,' and shoots her. I mean, he just points and shoots, no warning or nothing."

Chris paused, and I thought about Holt, playing me along. Marsh was wearing the gloves to avoid leaving fingerprints and to fool a later paraffin test on his hands. Which means that since Marsh fired the gun with the gloves on, there would have been evidence of that on the gloves themselves. Which Holt conveniently neglected to tell me.

Chris said, "You sure you want to hear all of this?"

"Yes."

He closed his eyes, but continued. "I go crazy, I mean, I'm already down on all fours, and he's treating me like shit and just shot the girl and probably's gonna shoot me. So I come up in a three-point stance, John, like back on the team, and I go at him, pumping like the coach said, all with the legs, not the head, the legs. I'm watching his stomach, so I can hit him solid, I don't see his face, but I pop him good and hard and I hear the gun go off again but I don't feel nothing and then I realize glass is breaking and I look up and he's . . . he's not there anymore." Chris shook his head vigorously, as though groggy after an impact. "The window's broken and he's gone."

"You left the gun there, Chris. My gun."

He opened his eyes and raised his hand. "John, I swear to God, I didn't know that. He didn't say nothing about it. And, anyway, I thought it went out the window with him."

"What did you do next?"

"I went over to Teri, to see if she was . . . but she was dead. Jeez, John, I could see her brains, like they were leaking. . . . In the closet, he's got the camera, some clothes, and a suitcase. All I was thinking is, 'He's got me on tape,' but I don't know nothing about those cameras, so I just yanked out the suitcase and opened it up. He had some kinda camera case in there, but it was closed and I didn't care, I just wanted to get out. I pulled his clothes off the hanger, hers too,

234

SWAN DIVE

I think, and I stuffed the clothes, the camera, and everything in the suitcase. I think I must have busted the legs on the tripod just to make it fit. I closed up the suitcase and threw my clothes on and got the hell out. I heard the elevator moving, so I used the stairs, but by the time I'd gone down maybe five flights I was breathing so hard I was afraid I'd pass out, so I went back into the hall on whatever floor it was and took the elevator back down to the lobby. Nobody was in it by then, I guess everybody was out and around the corner, gawking at the body. I just walked out and kept walking till I got to my car."

"What did you do with the suitcase?"

"I put it in the trunk and started driving, driving home, I mean. When I got partway, I realized I'd have to get rid of it, so I stopped at Revere Beach, the stretch with the wicked riptide. I ran out onto the sand with the thing and waited for two big beauties to roll in together, in the moonlight you could see them real clear. Then I heaved it as far as I could. It rode out but it floated at first. Jeez, John, I never fucking thought of that, it was so heavy, with the camera and all. But then it sank, lower and lower as it washed out, till I couldn't see it anymore, even with the moon. Then I went back to the car and drove home."

"Chris, you're the lawyer, but it seems to me that what happened in the room was self-defense. Why did you pack and run like that?"

"John, jeez, look at things the way they are, willya? I'm with a prostitute, and she gets shot, and I send the guy through the window. You think they're gonna believe me?"

"Maybe."

"So okay, so even if they do, the truth's worse than a good lie. I lose my ticket, John. The Overseers have to

235

pull my license, which is the only thing I got going for me. Also, the truth is that I'm everything that Eleni hates the most, the Greek husband who whores around, the difference being that she didn't just let herself go or something, she's sick and crippled in a way she can't control."

I stood up. "Chris, like I said, you're the lawyer. There are a lot of people screwed up in this, including me. You and I both know what you've got to do."

Chris brought the heels of his hands to his cheeks, then started rubbing under the eyes. "Right," he said quietly.

I drove toward Boston, finding it harder and harder to accept what Chris had told me. I parked the car behind the condo and walked the two blocks to Daisy Buchanan's, a popular sports bar on the corner of Fairfield and Newbury. I got there just early enough to get a seat, and I knew the bartenders who were on. They had some good new stories I hadn't heard, and the screwdrivers felt healthy as they raced one another down my throat and jostled in my stomach.

At some point, I had to wave for another drink, surprising because they're usually so attentive, the best in the city. I remember telling them that, that they were the best in the city. One asked me if I was walking or driving, and I sort of said walking. He said even so, just one more. I finished the drink, then had the pleasure of being escorted gently through the crowd of postcollege jocks and those who wished they were. They spared me the bouncer, telling me to be sure to come again. Place treats you with respect like that, of course you're going to come again.

I ricocheted off three trees and a lamppost covering the roughly two hundred yards back to the condo.

Anybody messing with me would have been one sorry fella, yessir. I got the keys out of the pocket on the third try and into the lock on the fourth, doing a little better upstairs at the apartment door. I kicked it shut, made it to the bedroom, and passed out across the mattress.

TWENTY-FOUR

I woke up Saturday morning, but just barely. The clock part of the radio said 11:40, meaning I must have slept through an hour's worth of alarm earlier. The head pounded, and my insides had that airy, rafting sensation you get from drinking on an empty stomach. I had no energy for running, so I toasted a couple of English muffins and drank a quart of ice water to rehydrate my system.

I showered, shaved, and dressed in clean sweatclothes, then went down to the car, started up, and drove to the Jamaicaway and around the trout pond. When I was with Empire, I did a lot of driving, and I found it could clear the head and focus the thinking. After five miles, my thinking was focused all right, but not helpfully.

My talk with Chris solved the killings, but Hanna and Vickie were left hanging in the breeze. Felicia had the money to buy off J.J., but Chris sure didn't and was on his way to definite disgrace and probable imprisonment. J.J. wouldn't understand why his drugs were backstroking to Portugal, and the cops weren't interested in restraining him.

I jammed on the brakes just in time to avoid a guy in a utility truck cutting into my lane. I hit the horn, and he threw me the finger as he turned, without any other signal, into a construction project. As I resumed speed, I watched him jounce over the rutted dirt driveway past some huge circular pipe sections that looked awfully familiar. I got my bearings and realized it was the same place J.J. and Terdell had taken me on Tuesday night.

That's when I got the idea. An idea that grew like Topsy.

It took me a while to measure time and distance by car. I ran each twice, then got back to the condo by 3:00. I dialed two numbers and got slightly different versions of "He's not here, you wanna leave a message?" I emphasized how important it was for each party to be available to hear from me at 8:00 P.M. I hung up and removed the phone jack from the wall to frustrate any premature return calls. Raiding the fridge, I ate all the absorptive foods I had. Then I nicked the nearly empty bottle of scotch from my landlord's liquor cabinet. I don't drink the stuff anymore, but it has a very recognizable smell.

I carried the bottle down to the car.

The first place I hit was a foundering blue-collar bar in Chelsea, the city just above Boston that those in favor of the manifest destiny of gentrification now call the "Near North Shore." I had three screwdrivers, listening to the owner describe the trouble he was having with his stepson. When I asked how bad he

239

was, the owner said, "Let me put it this way: he's the kinda kid, you saw his face on the side of a milk carton, you wouldn't feel so bad." I convinced him that it was the lawyers' fault, helping kids avoid juvenile detention and making them think they can get away with murder.

Next stop was a glitzy joint along the water in Revere, where a porky bartender with slicked-back hair and no sideburns told me I couldn't get in after six dressed the way I was. I explained to him that it was because of the lawyers, especially the young ones, pushing their noses into good old neighborhoods that had stood on their own for six generations. He agreed, treating me to one drink but then telling me I sounded like I'd already had enough for one afternoon. I thanked him for the drink if not the advice, and left.

The third place was a sticky-floored dive in Lynn, a city that's suffered so much arson that it's probably burned down three times over in the last ten years. The old woman working the wipe cloth said the flames nearly got her place twice, and she couldn't get no insurance and what the hell was she gonna do if they did torch it, anyway? I pointed out to her how the lawyers had manipulated it all, padding claims and sucking off what good people sweat their lives to get. She joined me in splitting half a bottle of Old Boston vodka on the rocks; I was able to dollop most of my share onto the floor when she wasn't looking. Exaggerating my departure, I gave her a kiss on the cheek that made her cackle. She said that I'd better watch for the cops if I was driving.

I edged another two miles north and parked on the beach at Nahant for two hours, watching an elderly couple and three kids, maybe grandchildren, move at the different paces of age along the waterline, stooping and whooping over shells and driftwood. I started up

again, skipping Swampscott and driving straight into
Marblehead. I stopped at a pay phone at 7:55 and
made both my calls. Each man was in and eager to
hear from me. I sounded as drunk as I could, giving
the second one directions just opposite of those I gave
the first. I told one good luck and the other to fuck off.
I made a third call, too, but when I heard the voice I
wanted, I just hung up.

I spent the next hour as obviously as possible in a
neighborhood bar on a street three blocks from the
harbor. I grossed out two nice women just because I
found out they were legal secretaries. The bartender
and a waiter had no trouble hustling me out the door,
though I did threaten them with immediate and costly
legal action.

I got back to the car and climbed in the driver's side.
Reaching under the seat, I retrieved the scotch. I
swished a bit like mouthwash around the teeth and
tongue and sprinkled the rest on the sweatshirt. I
tossed the bottle into an ash can and took a couple of
deep breaths. Then I walked to Felicia Arnold's house.

She answered the door with the same "Yes?" as she
had the phone. I leered at her and told her she was
beautiful. She scowled, and I asked if that wimp
Troller was there. I asked rather loudly, and that
brought Paulie-boy at a trot. He told me to shove off; I
asked him if he thought he was man enough to make
me.

Paulie let fly, and for the next three minutes or so,
he probably felt he was beating me to death.

T WENTY-FIVE

◆

For a while there, I thought I was going to have trouble with the Marblehead police. Not because of Felicia or Paul, who magnanimously told the two uniforms who responded to the scene that they didn't care to press charges. Not even for drunk driving, since the cops hadn't found me near my car. No, the problem was that the younger officer wanted to take me to the hospital. For observation and tests. Like a blood test, which would reveal my suspiciously low alcohol level. Fortunately, however, the older and cooler head prevailed, saying he'd "seen more guys beat up than Carter had Little Liver Pills, and this guy's just got his pride hurt, is all."

I contritely gave the older cop Murphy's name and office number in Boston to call to vouch for me. They drove me to their station and let me flop for the night in the holding cell, complete with sea breeze. It was nearly 6:00 A.M. Sunday, with a whole new shift on, when Holt and Guinness showed up.

"You know, Lieutenant, I've always wondered. Does every department order its interrogation rooms from the same catalog?"

Holt's eyelids had to stretch to climb down over his eyes, they were that bloodshot. Guinness made grumbling noises behind a huge Styrofoam cup of coffee in the corner. He hadn't offered me any.

Holt said, "For a guy who got the shit kicked out of him last night, you're pretty fucken chipper."

"I had it coming, Lieutenant. I got drunk, then got angry at the wrong guy."

"'Tender at the bar here, we already talked to him. He says you only had two drinks tops at his place."

I shook my head. "If that was all I had, I would have been all right. But I started at like four, down in Chelsea somewhere."

"Chelsea."

"Right. Guinness there knows where it is, right, Guinness? That's as far north as you've ever been, you told me."

Guinness just stared at me.

Holt said, "Where in Chelsea?"

I described the place, then took him through the rest of the odyssey, but vaguely, skipping around a little, then backing and filling.

Holt let out a breath. Guinness muttered, "Bullshit."

I said, "What's the problem?"

Holt said, "Your friends J.J. and Terdell."

I closed my eyes and said quietly, "Not Hanna and Vickie?"

Holt waited till I opened my eyes again. "No. J.J. and Terdell themselves."

"Dead?"

Guinness said, "You expect us to believe this is news to you?"

Holt silenced him with a look. "Cuddy, somebody set something up last night. We like you for it."

"Set up what?"

"The construction project where they worked you over. Somebody hit J.J. and Terdell there last night."

"How could you know where it was they worked me over?"

Guinness said, "Lieutenant. I gotta leave. I stay, I'm gonna clock him."

Holt said, "Go."

When the door closed, I said, "Where's Dawkins?"

"What's it to you?"

"Nothing. I just figured he'd be in on this with you."

"Maybe we couldn't reach him."

"I thought he was shadowing J.J. I thought that's how you all knew that J.J. had taken me to the construction site in the first place."

Holt didn't say anything.

I said, "Well, it's probably just Saturday night. Dawkins, I mean. You know, him having the weekend off and all."

After a few seconds, Holt said, "You gonna stick to this pub-crawling story?"

"It's no story, Lieutenant."

"I already got your gun, Cuddy, remember? Now I'm going after your investigator's license."

"On what ground? You know I didn't kill Marsh or Teri Angel. You're also gonna find out that I spent the afternoon intoxicating myself and the evening embarrassing myself. So now two pieces of shit turn up dead in some dirt pile that's not even in your jurisdiction. If I remember right, back from when we were discussing protection for Hanna and Vickie, you're real concerned about the limits of your jurisdiction."

Holt put both of his hands flat on the table and heaved himself up from the chair. "You get away with this, it's only gonna be because you didn't do it in Boston, get me?"

"Can I get out of here, at least?"

Holt said, "If the Marblehead cops don't want you, I sure as hell don't."

He opened the door and turned back to me. "You look like shit. I hope you're gonna clean up before the wake."

"Thanks, Lieutenant, but I'm afraid they're going to have to send J.J. and Terdell to the great beyond without me."

Holt looked at me kind of funny, then said, "You don't know, do you?"

"Know what?"

He gave me a smile, a heartless, hard smile. "Your friend, Christides the lawyer. He got up yesterday morning and ate his gun for breakfast."

I knocked on the front door of the house instead of the garage. Fotis answered. He didn't want to let me in, especially the way I looked. I made him understand that I thought Eleni would want to talk with me. He told me to wait and closed the door. He came back a minute later and told me to come in.

She was in the kitchen, sipping coffee, both hands around the cup. When she saw my condition, the tic in her eye cranked into high gear. Putting down the cup, she said something quickly to her cousin in Greek, and he left us.

"John, my God, your face and—"

"I'm all right, Eleni. Just a little fight."

She seemed to relax. "You heard."

"The police told me. Eleni, I'm so sorry . . ."

She dismissed that tack with a flick of her hand. "No, John, you do not be sorry. What happen here had to happen."

"I don't understand."

"He told me. After you leave Friday night. He finally come to me and told me. About the Marsh animal, about the drugs, about the . . . whore."

"Eleni, Chris was—"

"No! I do not want to talk about what he was. You I know, you a good man to help Hanna and the child, but that Marsh, he was a bad man. I could tell the first time I see him, and I tell you when I see you. But Chris does not kill Marsh because of what Marsh did, because of the pig he was. No, Chris kills Marsh because he was scared."

"I think you're being too hard on yourself. And on him. Chris was a good man."

"A good man does not visit the whores! I was a wife to Chris as long as I could. The . . . sickness takes me, John. Chris know what I know, that the days, there are not so many left. Still, he goes to the whore, like all the men in Greece I leave to come here."

"Eleni—"

"Chris was weak! Too weak to help the woman and child, too weak to be faithful to his wife, too weak even to do the right thing."

"What do you mean?"

"After you leave, and he tell me all the things, he lie awake, he cannot sleep, he say he will never sleep again. He say he will go crazy when the other lawyers find out what he did and take away his practice. He say he will go crazy in prison. He see the right thing, in front of him, and still he is too weak."

"I don't follow you."

"The suicide, John. The suicide, the right thing, and

he too weak even to do that. He so weak, in the end I have to help him."

I just stared down at her.

She said, "You a man with honor, John. You know what I mean."

God help me, I was afraid I did.

TWENTY-SIX

When you've been around death too much, I think you try hard to watch for encouraging signs of life. As I came over the Tobin Bridge, a dozen pleasure boats were making their way through the locks on the Charles River and out to the harbor. Winding along Storrow Drive, I paralleled couples strolling, kids playing, joggers striding. Even a few wind-skaters sailed by, twisting and dodging around the slower walkers and runners.

The day was brightening as much as I'd let it when I reached the condo's parking space. Along the street, an attractive woman was loading a picnic cooler into her hatchback, while a man holding his child's hand was stopped by a pair of nuns, traditionally hooded and graciously accepting the money he dropped into their woven basket. That struck the only jarring note; you'd think the church would have gotten its share at Mass in the morning.

I started walking around the building, but not fast enough. I could hear the nuns coming up behind me as I got to my front steps. One said, "Sir?"

I turned around and looked from the basket into Salomé's not quite angelic face. Niño glared at me from under the other hood, a .357 magnum with a three-inch barrel pointing out from where rosary beads should dangle.

Niño said, "Inside. Now."

"You give me a reason."

I said, "To shoot or not to shoot?"

Niño didn't answer. He stood in the center of my living room, headdress on the table but gun in his hand. His eyes could have pinned me to the couch. I heard Salomé at the refrigerator. She poked her head around the corner of the kitchen doorway, saying, "All you got is this Killian's shit?"

"Sorry."

She opened two, brought one in for Niño. She took a sip and a chair. Niño held the bottle by the neck and downed half of it.

He wiped his mouth and said, "I wanna hear just what the fuck you think you doing, man."

"You might want to sit down. It's going to take a while."

"Maybe you don't got a while. Talk."

I brought him up to date, quickly, since he already knew most of it.

"So Marsh use my Angel to set up the Greek lawyer."

"That's right."

Salomé said, "Fucken shithead."

"And you can't get J.J. to take the heat off the wife and kid."

"Uh-huh."

249

His voice rose. "So you fucken call me, and then call J.J., and tell both of us that his snow in one of those fucken pipes at the project."

"Yes."

"You motherfucken cocksucker! You set me up to get wasted, man."

"Not the way it worked out."

"Worked out? I start in that tunnel at the end you and me came out, just like you tell me to, and fucken Terdell, he coming from the other side, where him and J.J. have you before I save you *cojones*. I'm coming up on meeting him somewhere in the middle, and if it ain't for the fucken stink rolling ahead of him maybe five yards he waste me."

"I can't believe it was that close."

Niño slung the beer bottle at me in a whippy, underhanded way that made it carom off my collarbone and smash against the wall over my head, the red liquid staining as it ran down and along the woodwork. I rubbed the bone and didn't say anything about my security deposit.

"I gotta dive down when Terdell see me. He already have out this cannon, he start yelling my name. 'Niño, you fucken little shit, you was the one, you was the one,' and like that. Well, he get the two shots off, I don't even get the chance to say nothing, if I did I couldn't hear it 'cause the fucken noise from the shots like to break my ears open. Then J.J. coming up behind him, at the next junction in the tunnel. J.J. start spraying this Uzi all the fuck over, and maybe three slugs hit Terdell in the back. Fuck, Terdell not there, taking up so much of the tunnel, some of J.J.'s shots find me, you know it? So I low crawl to Terdell to get his piece, and somehow he stinking worse than when he was alive, musta had ten pounds of soul food shit coming out his ass when the muscles let go. J.J.

not too good with the Uzi in real life, probably bought it and took it out somewheres, learn how to shoot it but never seen no real combat with it, don't conserve his ammo."

"You caught him reloading?"

"Fucken A. He didn't even have the other load out, I bring up Terdell's piece, put one square in J.J.'s chest, man, he like explode. He tumble back, I wait on him, then check him out. Ter-mi-nat-ed, man."

I moved my head toward the gun pointing at me. "That's not Terdell's?"

Niño looked disappointed. "What you think, I got shit for brains? You think I carry away a piece that killed somebody?"

"What did you do with it?"

"I wipe it some, then put it back in Terdell's hand, press his fingers around it."

I thought for a second. "Which hand?"

Niño shook his head. "His shooting hand. *Madrón!*"

I said, "You didn't shoot your own gun in there?"

"Never got it out."

"Then the cops probably don't have the physical evidence to say anybody else was involved."

"The best I could do was leave it like maybe they had a business dis-a-gree-ment and did each other."

"With each other's weapons."

"I didn't know how much time I have, 'cause I didn't know if the cops still tailing J.J., 'cause I didn't know that you was inviting J.J., too."

"The main cop involved in the surveillance is a sergeant named Dawkins. He told me he was off this weekend."

"How come you didn't tell me, huh?"

"Somebody else was probably on. But you figure nobody saw you?"

251

Niño just said, "You fucken set me up, man. I saved you fucken life that night, and you fucken set me up."

"Put yourself in my position. You see any other way for me to get J.J. off the widow and the child?"

"You 'position,' huh? Back in the Nam, I had a lieutenant, fucken butter bar new guy, try to use me and my buddy to sucker some NVA one night. My buddy come back in a green bag, man. The butter bar got his ass reamed by a grenade somebody leave lying around."

"You told me you were the best, Niño, remember? King of the tunnel rats. I set it up, sure, but I set it up so I thought you'd take care of J.J. and Terdell no sweat."

"So you so thoughtful for me, I shouldn't just blow you away now?"

"No, you shouldn't."

"I still ain't heard no reason, man."

"In the Angel's apartment. You said you wanted the guy who killed her."

"You tell me Marsh kill her, and he's dead."

"Yeah, but J.J. was the real reason she was dead. You think Marsh would set up a crazy frame like he was working if he wasn't crazy himself from the drugs?"

Niño looked at me. "So I kill J.J., it's like me getting the guy who did the Angel, huh?"

"Right."

"Right, shit. If you right on that, then I oughta kill you now, 'cause without you rousting Marsh, he never get your gun or try to set you up or even fucken know you."

"Even without me in it, Hanna would have demanded the house, and Marsh would have tried to set up Chris through the Angel, just with another gun."

Niño seemed to think it over. "What if all that shit ain't enough reason?"

"Then try this. When you were driving me back Tuesday night, you said you figured you were better off me owing you a favor."

"So?"

"So now you're twice as well off as before. Now I owe you two favors, and you got an innocent woman and her daughter off J.J.'s hook."

Niño looked over to Salomé. I couldn't see her, but I heard her habit rustle as though she was gesturing.

Niño swung back to me and hitched at his robe near the crotch. "You got a set, man. You real lucky you draw a softhearted kind like me, you know it?"

I told him I knew it, and I meant it.

What's the occasion?

I fanned the long-stemmed roses in front of her headstone and straightened back up. I told her about confronting Chris, setting up Niño, and seeing Eleni.

Are you going to do anything about what Eleni told you?

"Like what? How much longer has she got? Besides, my credibility with the police is a little strained right now."

Not to mention you're feeling responsible.

"I don't. At least I don't now. When Holt told me, I thought, 'Jesus, it was me, me seeing Chris on Friday pushed him over the edge.' But not now."

I didn't mean so much that in particular. I mean in general, that it was you leaning on Marsh that started everything in motion.

"Niño already reminded me."

But you're wrong, you know?

"About what?"

253

*About you starting everything. Marsh was a louse
and Chris was weak, but you didn't make Hanna
marry one or Eleni marry the other.*

"Spouse-lock."

What?

I gave her Felicia Arnold's explanation.

Sounds like that could fit a lot of people's situations.

I didn't say anything.

John, don't you think it's time?

"I don't know."

Yes you do.

"Can I come up?"

She was wearing a loose-fitting Emack and Bolio Ice
Cream tee shirt, white tennis shorts, and sandals. She
took in my face. "Sure you weren't looking for the
first-aid station?"

I followed her up the stairs and into her apartment.
She motioned toward the couch and plopped herself
on a throw pillow.

"Nancy—"

"No, I want to get this straight, okay? So you listen
for a change. I don't want to hear what you've been
doing. I don't care what you think your reasons were. I
just want a decision from you, a decision about us and
about what you want us to be."

I looked down at her. The widely spaced bluer-than-
blue eyes, the upturned nose, the freckles sprinkled
from one cheekbone to the other.

"I've decided."

Always the lawyer, she kept her face neutral. "What
is it, then?"

I reached for her hand and inclined my head toward
the bedroom. "Let's," I said.

And so we did.

Pocket Books
Is Proud to Announce
the Publication of
Right to Die
A John Francis Cuddy Novel
by
Jeremiah Healy

Please turn the page for an
exciting preview of *Right to Die*.

PART OF IT STARTED AS A DARE, SORT OF.

I was thinking how Massachusetts is crazy about giving its citizens days off for events it's not really observing. For example, the third Monday in April is known as Patriots' Day. Supposedly, the Commonwealth closes down to honor those who served in war. Actually, it just excuses us from work for the Boston Marathon. I once warned a friend who'd called me from Texas, a diehard Dallas Cowboys fan, that he'd have a tough time arriving here on Patriots' Day. Awed, he said, "Y'all have a holiday for your football team?" In fact, Suffolk County alone sets aside March 17 for the Wearing of the Green. The Irish pols neutrally dubbed that one "Evacuation Day," commemorating the momentous afternoon the colonists kicked the British troops out of Boston harbor. I've never mentioned Evacuation Day to the Texan; I'm afraid of what he'd think we were celebrating.

Nancy Meagher said, "God, it's freezing!"

She was standing in front of me, my arms joined around her. Or, more accurately, around the teal L. L. Bean parka over bulky ski sweater over long johns that she was wearing. On a brutal Saturday evening in early December we were waiting with forty thousand other hardy souls on Boylston Street, across from the elevated patio of the Prudential Center, for the lighting of the Christmas tree. A fifty-foot spruce is given to the city of Boston each year by the province of Nova Scotia. The gift commemorates something else, but without a masking holiday, I can never remember what it is.

A man on an accordion platform was adjusting a camera and klieg lights. Several hundred smarter folks watched from inside the windows of the Pru Tower or the new Hynes Convention Center. The smell of sausage and peppers wafted from somewhere near the Paris Cinema.

Nancy said, "Unconscionable."

"Sorry?"

"It is unconscionable not to start on time when it's this cold."

Hugging Nancy a little tighter, I looked around at our immediate neighbors. High school and college kids, not dressed sufficiently for the temperature, stamping their feet and stringing together ridiculous curses in the camaraderie of youth. Parents more my age, rubbing the mittened hands of their kids or wiping tiny red noses with wads of tissues pulled from pocket or handbag. A couple of cops in earmuffs, standing stoic but watchful. The crowd was well behaved so far, but occasionally you could hear coordinated shouting. If the Japanese restaurant behind and below us could have put up sake to go, they'd have made a fortune.

The weather really afflicted Nancy, but I was wearing just a rugby shirt under my coat and over my corduroy pants. Some Vikings must have come over the wall in my ancestors' part of County Kerry, because I rarely feel the winter.

To take Nancy's mind off it, I said, "You know, this is where the finish line used to be."

"The finish line?"

"Of the marathon."

No response.

I said, "The *Boston* Marathon?"

She cricked her neck to frown at me. Black hair, worn a little longer since autumn, wide blue eyes, a sprinkling of freckles across the nose and onto both cheeks. "Not all of us are day-labor private investigators, John Cuddy."

"Meaning?"

"Meaning I've lived in this city all my life, and I've never once seen the marathon in person."

"You're kidding?"

"It's too cold to kid."

"But the marathon's a holiday."

Nancy shrugged off my arms. "When I was little, traffic was too snarled to come over here from South Boston. When I was in law school, I thanked God for the extra day and studied."

"Nance, even the courthouse closes for the marathon. What's your excuse now?"

"I never knew anybody stupid enough to run that far."

"It's not stupid."

"It is."

"Is not."

She almost smiled. " 'Tis."

" 'Tain't."

"I suppose you think you could run it."

"I suppose I could."

"John, you're too big."

"Six two and a little isn't too big."

"I meant you're too heavy. The guys they show on TV are string beans."

"One ninety and a little isn't that heavy. Besides, I'd train down for it."

"John, anyway you're too . . ."

Nancy tried to swallow that last word, but I'd already heard it.

I said, "Too what?"

"Never mind."

"Too old, is what you said. You think I'm too old to run the marathon."

There was a feedback noise from an amplifier. Some "older" men were fiddling with a tall microphone on the patio under the tree. Then a male voice came over the public address system. "On behalf of the Prudential Center, I would like to welcome you to—"

The rest of his comments were drowned out by the swelling cheer of the crowd.

Over the roar I said into Nancy's ear, "Now it's down the street a couple of blocks."

"What?"

"I said, now it's down—"

"What is?"

"The finish line of the marathon. It used to be just about where we're standing. But when Prudential decided to scale back its operations here, the John

Hancock agreed to sponsor the race and moved the finish line down almost to the Tower." I pointed to the Hancock, a Boston landmark of aquamarine glass now known more for its sky deck than for the four-by-ten windows that kept sproinging out and hurtling earthward just after it was built.

Nancy didn't turn her head. "Fascinating. And still stupid."

At the mike a priest delivered a longish invocation. I let my eyes drift over to the Empire Insurance building. My former employer. I don't think Empire ever sponsored so much as a Little League team.

The priest was followed by our Mayor Flynn, who was blessedly brief in his remarks. Then the premier of Nova Scotia began an interminable speech that I couldn't follow. Nancy huddled back against me.

About ten feet from us, four guys wearing Boston College varsity jackets started a chant. "Light the fuckin' tree, light the fuckin' tree."

I laughed. Nancy muttered, "You're contemptible."

Finally, Harry Ellis Dickson, the conductor emeritus of the Boston Pops Orchestra, had his turn. He introduced Santa to much squealing and wriggling among the kids, many of whom were hoisted by dads and moms onto shoulders. Then Harry led the crowd through several carols. "O Come, All Ye Faithful," "Joy to the World," "Hark, the Herald Angels Sing." Everybody knew the first few lines, most of us dah-dah-ing the rest.

Between carols Nancy sighed. "We've become a one-stanza society."

Two slim figures in oddly modified Santa outfits danced up the steps of the patio.

Nancy said, "Who are they supposed to be?"

"Santa's eunuchs."

Again she shrugged off my arms. "I take it back. You're beneath contempt."

After a few more carols the star on top of the tree was lit, setting off a reaction in the crowd like the first firecracker on the Fourth of July. The long vertical strips of lights came on next. Then, beginning at the top, sequential clumps mixing red, blue, green, and yellow flashed to life, more a shimmer than individual bulbs, until the magic had hopped down the entire tree.

We finished with a universal "Silent Night," the crowd breaking up while the last notes echoed off the buildings.

"John! Gee, how long's it been?"

Tommy Kramer forgot to take the napkin off his lap as he rose to greet me. It fell straight and true to the floor. Only heavy cloth for Sunday brunch at Joe's American Bar & Grill.

"Tommy, good to see you."

He sat back, crushing a filterless cigarette in an ashtray but not noticing the napkin between his penny loafers. Moving upward, the flannel slacks were gray, the oxford shirt pale blue, the tie a Silk Regent with red background, and the blazer navy blue. Dressing down, for Tommy.

I took in the room's detailed ceilings and mahogany wainscoting, pausing for a moment on the bay window overlooking Newbury Street. The shoppers below bustled around half an hour before the boutiques would open for Christmas-season high rollers. We had a corner all to ourselves, the yuppies holding off until after twelve, when the booze could start to flow.

Tommy's rounded face seemed to lift a little, making him look younger. "You know, my old law firm used to own this place."

"I didn't know. The Boston one, you mean?"

"Right, right. Firm got started before the turn of the century, one of the first in the city to decide to make a Jew a partner. When word leaked out about that, the downtown eating clubs very politely told the firm's established partners, 'Well, you understand, of course, that we can't serve him here.' At which point the partners basically looked at each other, said 'fuck you' to the clubs, and bought a restaurant downtown for lunch meetings and this one here in Back Bay for dinner."

"So they could eat where they wanted."

"With whoever they wanted, including the new Jewish partner."

"The firm still run the place?"

"No, no. Sometime after I went out on my own in Dedham, they sold it. Back then, though, it was heady stuff for a young lawyer like me to be able to walk into one of the finest restaurants in Boston and be treated like the king of Siam."

"Your practice going well?"

"The practice? Oh, yeah, yeah. Couldn't be better. We're at eight attorneys now with the associate we brought in last week. Evening grad from New England."

Nancy's alma mater. "Kathy and the kids?"

"Terrific. She's gone and got her real estate ticket. Salesman, not broker yet, but that'll come in time. She's showing real estate all over town and having a ball. Slow market, like everywhere, but she knows the neighborhoods and the schools. Jason's on the wrestling team, Kit's doing indoor—oh, I get it. If everything's okay on the practice and home fronts, how come I drag you in here on ten hours notice?"

"Something like that."

A waitress in a tux came to the table and asked if we'd like to order. Both of us went with orange juice, eggs Benedict, and a basket of muffins.

When she was beyond earshot, Tommy said, "It's not for me. It's for somebody I owe."

Tommy's oblique way of reminding me that I still owed him for a favor.

"I'm listening."

He coaxed another cigarette from the Camel soft pack. "Okay if I . . . ?"

"The smoke doesn't bother me if the surgeon general doesn't bother you."

A match from the little box on the table flared, giving Tommy for an instant the look of a combat soldier, the curly hair still full enough to mimic a helmet. "Who would've thought, twenty, thirty years ago that someday you'd have to ask permission to light up?"

When I didn't say anything, he took a deep draw, then put the cigarette down, using the thumb and forefinger of his other hand to tweezer bits of tobacco from his tongue. "The guy approached me because he's not a lawyer himself, but he wants confidentiality in sounding you out."

"Tommy, the licensing statute requires me to

maintain the confidentiality of whatever the client tells me."

"Right, right. And this guy knows that. It's just . . . well, he wouldn't exactly be the client."

"Somebody wants to talk with me—"

"Wants me to talk with you—"

"But this somebody wouldn't be my actual client?"

"Right."

Our orange juice arrived. I sipped it. Fresh-squeezed, not from concentrate. Like the difference between chardonnay and Ripple. "Okay, I'm still listening."

"A friend of this guy is getting threats."

"Threats. Like over the telephone?"

"Like through the mail. Cut-and-paste jobs using words from magazines."

"The friend of the guy been to the police?"

"Not exactly."

"What exactly?"

"The secretary of the friend of the guy tried—"

"Tommy, this is getting a little out of hand. How about some real names."

He turned that over, shook his head. "How about some titles to make it easier?"

"Titles."

"Until you know whether you're interested or not."

"Okay. Titles."

Tommy pulled on the Camel, wisps of smoke wending out of his nostrils. "The guy I owe, let's call him the Activist. His friend who's getting the threats, let's call the friend the Professor. The Professor's secretary—"

"Tried going to the police."

"Right."

"And?"

"And the cops can't do much. I'm not into criminal law, but I'm assuming they checked the notes for fingerprints or postmarks and all, and came up empty."

"So you want me to do what?"

"I want you to talk to the Activist and the Secretary as my agent, if you're willing."

"As your agent."

"Right."

"Talk to them about what, bodyguarding the Professor?"

"No, no. She—they can talk to you more about that."

"Tommy . . ."

"Look, John, I know this sucks a little, but like I said, I owe the guy."

"The Activist."

"Right."

"Can you at least tell me how you owe this guy?"

Tommy took another puff. "When I was with that firm in Boston, they were real civil rights conscious."

"Good thing to be."

"Yeah, well, most of us young associates signed up as volunteers, whatever, for different causes through the BBA."

"Boston Bar Association?"

"Right, right. I drew . . ."

He stopped, took a puff out of sequence. "I drew this activist, and after I helped him out a couple of times, he started throwing a lot of business my way, business I really needed once I broke off on my own."

"Activist, Professor, Secretary."

"Huh?"

"Tommy, these don't sound like people who need the layers of confidentiality you're throwing up around them."

"John, that's kind of their business, don't you think?"

"Tommy, you want me to meet with them, it's kind of my business, don't you think?"

He put a casual look on his face, checking the room. "This activist, John, he's . . . Alec Bacall."

"Rings a bell somewhere."

"He's a gay activist, John."

Bacall. Majored in housing and employment rights, minored in AIDS issues. "Tommy, the professor here. Maisy Andrus?"

He flinched. "Keep your voice down, okay?"

"The right-to-die fanatic."

Tommy reddened. "She's not—" He caught himself speaking too loudly, our waitress thinking he meant her to come over. Tommy shook her off with an apologetic smile.

More quietly, Tommy said to me, "She's not a fanatic, John. She was a professor of mine, back in law school."

"At Boston College?"

"Right, right. Before she went over to Mass Bay."

I waited for Tommy to say something about my year as a student at the Law School of Massachusetts Bay. He didn't.

I said, "So Andrus was a professor of yours."

"And she helped me get that first job, at the law firm. Letter of recommendation, couple of phone calls, I found out later."

"So you owe her too."

"Yeah."

"And now she's being threatened."

Tommy ground out the cigarette. "Right."

"And she turns to you to turn to me."

"No, no, Alec—Bacall—is the one who called me."

I sat back. Watching him.

"What's the matter, John?"

"Quite a coincidence."

"Huh?"

"You contacting me to maybe help these people who preach the quick-and-happy ending."

Tommy looked very uncomfortable. Which was as good an answer as my next question could bring.

"John, look—"

"Tommy. I lost Beth to cancer, slowly. Bacall pushes the right to die for AIDS victims, Andrus casts a wider net. I'm the first one you think of?"

"John, I'm sorry. I should have . . . Look, I owe these people. From a long time ago, but I owe them. I once mentioned to Alec about Beth. Not directly, just that I could understand his position because I had a good friend who became a private investigator partly because his wife died. I never used your name or Beth's, it was just . . ."

"An example."

"Yeah. I'm sorry, but yeah. Then Alec calls me yesterday, and the guy's got a mind like a steel trap. He remembers me mentioning your situation, John. And he asks me to ask you."

Picking up my orange juice, I pictured Tommy dropping everything to help me with Empire and with Beth. To Tommy bailing me out when I was filling a hospital bed, a bullet hole in my shoulder and a skeptical D.A. on my neck.

"I'll talk to them."

"Great, great. Uh, John?"

"Yes."

"Today maybe?"

Nancy was at work, catching up on some research. After one more stop in the neighborhood, I'd be free for the afternoon.

"Two o'clock, Tommy. My office on Tremont Street."

"Alec said he'd be at the professor's house, so I'll call them now. I really appreciate this, John."

Getting up, Tommy got his feet tangled in the napkin and nearly fell into our waitress and eggs Benedict.